MetaMorphosis

Anthony Murkar

ISBN: 0-9812441-1-4
ISBN-13: 978-0-9812441-1-2

MALITOPRESS

Printed in the United States of America

*This book is dedicated to my mother,
and also to all of those who read it. I sincerely hope
that it makes a difference in your lives.*

CHAPTER ONE

Embarking

The streets were busy with too many people, some shopping for the upcoming holiday, some going to the show, some just out for a walk. This was the case with Jasper; he was out for a walk, one which so far had served him no purpose but to stretch his weary legs. His hair was slightly long, greasy, and dark brown. He was unshaven, but oddly enough he wore decent clothes—more decent than usual, anyways, though they were still rather ragged and poor looking. It was dark outside now, probably about eight at night he guessed, and the clouds slowly obscured his view of the moon. No stars were visible; the light pollution from the city was far too great to allow them to shine through.

Jasper hated how he couldn't see the stars; when he was a child, before he had come to the city, he used to stare up at the stars all the time. He grew up on a farm which was many hours away from where he now stood, and even though it was part of a small town, there were not enough lights to blot out all of the stars. There were magnificent red and maroon colors in the sky and thousands of stars. Jasper had always attempted to count as many as he could, but he never managed to count them all—he had always lost count or lost sight of where he was counting. Often in the summer, he and his brother would set a tent up outside

1

and stay out looking at the stars late into the night, before getting scared and going inside instead of sleeping in the tent. He brought his mind back to the world that currently surrounded him, noticing all of the worldly appendages that polluted the streets.

Jasper noticed a scalper selling tickets to the show. It wasn't so common to see one for a show in that area, since many of the tickets for shows like these were often sold out to people who used them only as a tool for discussing business with potential clients and the like. Once more he remembered his childhood; he was thinking about how he had been in school. He had never particularly liked school, though everybody said it was good for him and he needed it. Jasper always struggled with the work given to him and he found that the schools were stifling places—he was never bullied or anything, sometimes the other way around—but there were always people who did it on a regular basis to the same people and he, solely out of fear for his own position, found it difficult to speak up about it. He was concerned about his own welfare and telling a teacher would have meant certain death to his social life.

He had always been deeply concerned with his position on the social ladder at his school. To be "cool," to be part of the "in" crowd. Jasper was the kind of person, back then and even somewhat now, who would insult a friend in front of others to make himself feel important or better than them. It had lost him several friends over the years, one of which was now a partner at a large law firm who refused to speak with him. When he was in school, he found the building and atmosphere extremely stifling. He had really longed to get out of there, but he wasn't permitted to leave. Nobody was. He had been the social butterfly in school, but now it did him no good. Sociability was not a marketable skill unless it was paired with knowledge or other skills.

Jasper stopped at the corner of the theatre and leaned up against the brick. He removed a cigarette from his pocket and struck a match. He was not financially comfortable—in fact, he was poor. He had to feed his addictions, though, and smoking was one of them. He lit his cancer stick and puffed away on the corner. Then he cocked his head backwards and blew a smoke ring into the air. Watching the smoke ring made him think about what he wanted to do with his life. There were so many expectations of him, none of which were fulfilled as of yet. Society demanded so much that he just couldn't grant. Really, he just wanted to be that smoke ring, to float peacefully in the cool night air, to be stress free. Still, though, the smoke ring had expectations. It wasn't a smoke ring unless it kept it's shape. He hadn't kept his shape, though.

Perhaps, Jasper thought, it's like everything else. It had a beginning and an end, and it changed its form throughout the course of its life. The smoke ring twisted in the air and, eventually, it disappeared and faded back into a part of the world from which it had come. Averting his eyes from the smoke ring, Jasper looked to his left. The scalper was still trying to sell tickets to the show, which was starting in mere minutes.

The scalper looked like the type of person who would do anything for a dollar, the type who would pinch every penny necessary to get his money. Oddly enough, those were the type of people Jasper often observed as the least happy. That's not to say that Jasper was happy, though. He, too, had his issues—in fact, he had many of them.

"Hey, you!" The scalper called. Jasper stared at him quizzically. "Yeah, you, come here!" Jasper leaned his head back down and looked in the direction of the scalper before walking over to the other end of the old brick building where he was standing. He edged his way around a small group of people huddled together, careful not to slip off the curb into the street which was packed with taxis. The group of people looked like a family, and they were lined up for the show. The show must have been starting really soon, Jasper assumed, because people were lined up. *Typical for a penny pincher like that to be selling tickets right up until the show starts*, Jasper thought. He moved through the now extensive line of people, repeating, "Excuse me, pardon me," as he advanced toward the Scalper.

As he finished pushing his way through the crowd, the scalper held up a ticket. "Hey," he said, "I've got one left, and I need to sell it. You willing?" Jasper looked at the ticket that had been shoved in his face. He had nowhere to be, but it was probably an expensive show. "How much?" he asked.

"The show's starting in less than ten minutes, people are lined up, and I probably won't sell this ticket if you don't buy it. Make an offer." Jasper considered it. He hadn't been to a show in a long time. Not since he was a child, actually.

Jasper's mother used to take him to shows often; to the opera, to the symphony, and to plays. His favourite was the symphony. He had always wanted to learn to play the violin but never got around to it. He couldn't afford to do it now, anyway. Perhaps, he thought, one day I'll learn. Jasper reached down and felt for his wallet in his left pocket. He had no wallet though; he had forgotten that he'd pawned it days ago for a package of cigarettes. He pulled out a crumpled ten-dollar bill and said to the scalper, "This is all I have." He really did want to go in, to bring him back to the days when he was a child when he would sit in the crowd with his mother and father and listen to the symphonies and watch the plays. It would, perhaps, give him some gumption to get out and do something. Or, at least, to break his addictions.

The scalper looked over the ten-dollar bill and, then, he took it. "Alright," he said, "I probably won't get better than that at this point. Here." He handed Jasper a ticket, and walked off. Jasper hadn't even taken the time to look at what show was playing before purchasing the ticket. He had not even feigned interest in it until he began to recall his childhood. Looking down at the ticket, he checked to see the name of the play. There was no name on the ticket, though. It looked real; he assumed it wasn't a fake, but he couldn't find any indication of what the play might be about on the ticket. He felt cheated, but decided to ask someone near him.

"Excuse me," he said, tapping a tall, elderly man with a peppery mustache on the shoulder. "Could you tell me what this play is about?" The man ignored him. It seemed as if everyone was ignoring him. He took a place in line and stood there, waiting for his admission to the show. The line was slow moving, and it seemed to take forever. In fact, by standing in the group he had moved less than three meters ahead in over five minutes. It was cold out, and he wished that he had something more to wear. He couldn't help but notice that the street had become empty of everybody except for those waiting patiently in the lineup. There was nothing, not even cars, which was extremely odd for this place. He had never seen the street here empty of vehicles, let alone people.

He was lost in his own wonder when he felt a tap on his shoulder. With a start, he turned to see an old woman standing there. She was quite wrinkled and had white hair. She carried a green and red plaid umbrella, which he now noticed was what she had tapped him with. She wore a grey suit jacket with a plaid vest beneath and a matching skirt. Jasper noticed that the umbrella was wet, and so was his shoulder now from it, but he could not think of a place from which the water

6

could have come. It had not rained there in over a week. After a short pause, he realized that he had been staring confusedly at her, and she too had been staring at him with an authoritative look on her face.

"Young man," she said to Jasper, "what are you doing standing in this line?" He was confused at the question asked to him by this old woman, in her thick English accent. What else could he be doing? "I am waiting for the show," he snapped, "why else would I be here?" He was upset that his only jacket was now dirty and wet on the shoulder. He frowned at her.

"Now, don't give me that face. Why are you lining up for the show? Just because everybody else is doing it doesn't mean you have to." He didn't understand. "Listen," she said, "you're standing in line because everybody else is, not because you want to see the show."

"This is absurd," he retorted sharply, "I'm just standing in line. What have I done wrong?"

She frowned at *him*, now. "You're not getting it, sonny. Come on, I'll show you."

She took him by the arm and pulled him out of line. "No, I'll lose my spot!" he said. It was too late, though, and the person behind him advanced to take his place, and the rest of the line followed. "Don't be such a fuss," she said, "come with me." She took him by the arm and smiled as they walked along the long crowd of people. "Look at them all," she said. "not moving anywhere. The whole lot of them, just standing there. It sickens me." Jasper felt odd, walking arm in arm with this odd woman down the sidewalk. "I'm sorry Jasper," she said, "but you weren't moving anywhere and I couldn't help but give you a hand."

"How did you…?" he started, but was cut off by her pressing her finger to his lips and saying "Shhhhh…"

The crowd had ignored the two of them so far; it was as if they weren't there. Jasper felt odd but didn't question it. As they neared the front of the lineup, the woman pointed to the man in the front of the line arguing with the person taking tickets. "There's your problem," she said, "it's that one. The whole group moves at the speed of the slowest member. It's a pity people don't just...*go around.*" She beckoned Jasper to follow her into the theatre. At the front of the theatre, he noticed there were two extremely long lines, one to the left and one to the right, which extended along the entire length of the building. Neither of them were moving particularly fast. There was, however, a third door between the two lineups where few people stood. Each person in that line went through fairly quickly, and the woman led Jasper to that door. "Excuse me, Madam," the ticket man at the door said, "but aren't you a little old for this show?"

He was wearing a red and gold outfit, a matching hat, and was holding a large pile of ticket stubs. His face looked warm, not like the kind of person who would say something like that at all.

"Well," the old woman replied, "I don't think there's such a thing as 'too old.' I'm old, but not 'too' old. You're never too old to learn and to have new experiences." She smiled at him, and the ticket man took her ticket and ripped off the stub. "Well, as long as you think you can handle it." He gave a smile back, and the woman proceeded to tug Jasper into the theatre, laughing a little at what the ticket man had said to her.

"There, that wasn't so bad, was it?" She said to Jasper.

"Wait," Jasper said to her, "he didn't take my ticket!" She gave another chuckle. "You don't need a ticket to this show, everyone's welcome." Jasper felt cheated, paying for a ticket that there was no charge for. He soon forgot about it, though; Jasper had become infatuated with the sights and sounds of the theatre, and he didn't feel that losing money was a great loss. He could have lost a million dollars at this point and he wouldn't have minded.

Jasper had been in this particular theatre on three separate occasions, the most memorable being the last. It was the last day he saw her before…Jasper withdrew his thoughts from that painful memory, forgetting it as fast as he had remembered it. He felt a tug on his arm again and was pulled by the woman through a doorway, which led to the seating area. They were on the second level—the lower level was down a flight of stairs from the main entrance. "Look at it all." The woman stared nostalgically at the crowd of people now filling the seats. "They just…come and go. And that's it, that's all they do. They follow what everybody else does, and then they end up moving forward so

9

slowly like the people in that lineup. It's a pity they don't get more into the show. They just watch it go by instead of living it and really...*experiencing* it." She took a deep breath and held onto Jasper's arm. "Here's your seat, sonny, I have to be off now. My seat is on the other side of this place, and the show will be starting soon." Jasper took his seat, and the woman walked out through the swinging door that they had come in through.

The door now swung rapidly, and the hall was filling with men in suits and dress jackets and women in magnificent dresses. The symphony could be seen practicing before the stage. Jasper leaned back comfortably in his chair and stared at the ceiling, which looked as if it were laden with all the stars of the sky. The theatre continued for several minutes to fill with people, and then the lights dimmed and Jasper sat up. The seats beside him were empty, though he could not see any other empty seats. It was now quite dark, and the violins struck a long single note all at once, just before the curtains were drawn back to reveal the stage.

A man dressed rather clumsily, looking almost homeless, stood at center stage. The lights centered on him. Jasper guessed that the man's outfit was a costume for the show, which intrigued Jasper. He looked to be about middle aged and was holding a microphone, its black cord dangling over the front edge of the stage. He looked as if he hadn't shaved in a while. His eyes were brilliant green and, even from that far back, Jasper could see them. It began to feel hot in the room, and

Jasper felt stifled. It felt as if the theatre was closing in on him. He felt hot and sweaty and then cold. His vision blurred, then darkened to the point where he almost couldn't see at all. The only thing he could see was the man at centre stage, whom his eyes were locked on.

"Good evening, Everybody!" The man yelled. He had a brilliant voice, one that carried throughout the theatre like waves in the ocean. "We have prepared a brilliant show for you tonight!" The crowd clapped, and the man gave a maniacal smile. "So now," he spoke, "as you view this masterpiece, we hope you become so immersed in it that it *becomes you!*" As he spoke the last words, the violins began to play a strong, high note. He began to sing a loud song, which shook the very supports of the theatre. When he quieted from his solo, the crowd clapped all at once. Some stood in their seats.

The bass began to pluck, the violins to sing, and the horns to blow. The chimes chimed, and the piano played as the orchestra played an extraordinary accompaniment to the tenor's singing. It was an odd show, one that Jasper had never seen, and he could even have sworn that he heard his name mentioned in the song on two different occasions. The curtains closed once more, and the lights brightened a bit as the orchestra changed their sheet music and the stage was rearranged.

CHAPTER TWO

The Battle Begins

In a few moments, the curtains opened again, and there was a group of soldiers tightly meshed together in a bunker among an extremely realistic looking battlefield. One yelled, "Jasper, get to cover!" Looking down, Jasper realized that he was dressed in a uniform. He looked once more around him, and he was onstage. The faces of the audience grew progressively farther from him, until they were literally only visible in the sky. The battlefield was now quite real, and it was expanding outwards around him, off into the distance as far as the horizon—possibly even farther. There were clouds overhead, and his ears were filled with the sound of nearby explosions and gunfire. The stars to the stage were now gone, as was the curtain, and the only remnants of the theatre that remained was the crowd staring down at him intently, though he could not reach them. He was standing in mud, and there were craters from artillery fire scattered around the stage. The bunker was now made of concrete. He stood there in shock, not moving, until an artillery round landed just meters from him and sent the remains of another soldier in all directions. He dived into an artillery hole as shots fired around him, kicking up bits of mud in his face.

"Where am I?!" he screamed. He heard the voices from the bunker once more. "Jasper, get to cover! Now!" His head was poking out of the crater, and he could see smoke and explosions on the horizon. There was a city not too far off, though right here it was all mud. The ground was covered with brass bullet casings. Another shot near his right hand sent mud up into his face, and he spit as mud and sand landed in his mouth. He rubbed his eyes, which were now sore and red. He felt tired.

"Come on, Jasper!" his comrades yelled. Standing up from the bunker, Jasper grabbed his rifle, which had been sitting on the ground next to him, and rushed toward the bunker. He dived as an artillery round struck near him once more, which knocked him off his feet. He landed face first in the mud. Standing once more, he ran toward the bunker which was surrounded by a barbed-wire fence. Diving over the fence, he landed in a shallow trench and crawled his way into the bunker.

He was breathing heavily, and his face, whatever was not covered by mud, was red. Looking at himself in a piece of broken glass, he looked older than before. Not much older, maybe a few years. His heart thumped viciously as his comrades surrounded him. "Jasper, you ok?"

"Where am I?!" he screamed. He sunk down into the ground. "Oh shit," one said, "this can't be good." Another grabbed his face and slapped it, saying, "Jasper, snap out of it!" He looked around. There was a dead man in the corner of the bunker, and he could barely hear over the sound of machine-gun fire. There

13

ANTHONY MURKAR – METAMORPHOSIS

was a mounted gun pointing out of a hole in the bunker wall, through which it fired at the enemy.

A soldier rushed in and yelled, "guys, we have to get out of here! Oh damn, Jasper! What happened?"

"I think he's in shock!" yelled a soldier with a red cross on his helmet. They all wore old looking uniforms, made of a heavy canvas material. It felt cold and hot to Jasper at the same time, and his lungs seemed to close up on him and stop him from breathing. Another slap to the face brought him back to reality. "Jasper, come on, we have to get out of this bunker!" one said. Jasper stood, not bothering to question, and leaned against another soldier who helped him up.

A map was produced and a heavy, grizzly-looking soldier took control. "Alright," he said, "this is where we are, and this is where we need to be." He pointed to a small town on the map, which Jasper guessed was what he mistook for a city. "We move as a group. We'll go in between those two posts."

"Why are we doing this?" Jasper asked. "What is the point of this?" The group all turned at once and stared at him, looming over him like giants.

"What do you mean?" another soldier asked. This one was a smaller man wearing glasses.

"This place, what am I doing here?" The soldiers continued to stare at him, until one spoke.

"We need to save as many as we can from their atrocities, Jasper, that's our mission. This whole goddamn war. We have to stop them, they're killing whoever gets in their way. It's not right."

Someone gave Jasper a slap on the shoulder. "Don't worry, man, it'll work and we'll get out of here. Now let's go."

Jasper could still hear the symphony strings plucking, and as he looked out toward the audience, he saw them all, blankly staring at them. They weren't moving or responding, just watching intently as the battle raged on before them. The audience was dark, and all he could see were their faces illuminated by a pale light. It was dark on the field now, and fog occluded their vision as they crawled through the mud. Jasper looked out toward the orchestra, who were facing the stage and playing music to follow. Suddenly, the instruments stopped, and he could hear the string playing a quiet high note, which gradually became stronger and stronger until it became a low note, accompanied by the bass.

A large, grey automobile passed by them, lying in the mud. It was night, now, and it was completely dark. They were hidden there in the mud, but the truck narrowly missed them, passing through the mud. They had crawled a far distance now, and the bunker was no longer visible. The audience, however, was still the same distance away, always watching. Jasper couldn't take it any more; he yelled out to the audience "Help me, what are you doing?! Why are you just watching?!" The audience didn't move, though. The truck stopped, it's big black tires not moving in the mud, as one of the other mud-covered soldiers dived on top of him and covered his mouth.

The truck engine stopped, and the vehicle heaved a great puff of grey smoked from the pipe above the cab. He could hear the door creaking, and Jasper lay still. None of them dared to move. The door slammed shut, and all that could be heard was the sound of footsteps through the mud. A rat waddled across the ground past Jasper's face, and he stifled his fear by closing his eyes. He was sweating heavily, now, even though it was quite cold. He could see his breath in the air, and so he held it in as long as he could to both hide his breath and remain as quiet as possible. The steps grew closer and closer, walking around amongst the bodies lying on the ground.

Jasper could hear the squish of boots in the mud near his face and could actually feel the boot expelling mud into his face as it stomped down at the tip of his nose. He held in his breath as long as he could, but he could not do it for much longer. The foot stayed there for a moment, before the steps finally moved away. He let out a little bit of his breath by accident as the footsteps drew quiet, and they stopped. Jasper's heart pounded as he held his breath. He caught a glimpse of a soldier dressed in a black overcoat with a hat bearing a red emblem walking back towards him. The soldier peered around, looking for the source of the sound.

Looking at the soldier, Jasper was shocked and frightened by the sight of him. He bore no face; it appeared as if all of the normal facial features had been ripped off. There was just a scarred mass of flesh there, nothing more. Jasper had to close his eyes to keep himself from screaming. It was a monstrous being, an abomination of a man. Jasper could barely keep himself from yelling. Inside his mind, he was screaming until he ran out of breath, breathing deeply and then screaming again and again. The sight of that face made his skin tighten and shiver. The face haunted his mind. The thing stood there for a long time—it seemed like hours to Jasper—before the faceless soldier finally departed and went back to the vehicle. The low, yet loud, rumble of the engine, which now excreted more black smoke, could be heard disappearing into the distance as Jasper's group began to continue crawling through the mud towards their destination. Jasper, though, was still haunted by the image of that monstrous thing that had been searching for them. He was afraid to even think what they would do to them if they were captured.

The group of soldiers continued to crawl along for a long time, what seemed, to Jasper, like hours. He could feel the audience still staring at him, but they were not in sight. He felt, though, as if he was being watched, and he knew they were there. The very idea of what had happened boggled his mind. *How did I get here?* He wondered. *Where am I?* They continued to crawl through the mud among bodies and wretched barbed wire, which had rusted. He could barely see for the fog that lay heavily on them. The fog, obscuring his vision, was something he had always liked. He wanted to…hold onto it, though it was not tangible. He wanted to sit there, hiding from the world, whenever he was in the fog.

There used to be fog like this often at his Grandparents' house in England. He had been given the opportunity to go there almost every fall as a child, and he could still smell the dead leaves as he would sit out in the fog on the lawn every morning when it was there. He used to sit on the stone fence, which had been crumbling and falling apart for as long as he could remember, and just stare out into the fog. There was nothing there, nothing of any importance. It was just comfort for him. He knew, though, that he would always have to leave that comfort for the warm house because, no matter how comfortable he felt there, it was cold and damp, and he would catch a cold out there. There were always warm scones with cream or butter waiting for him inside.

They crawled silently onwards through the night, all night in fact. They could not stop for sleep, though Jasper didn't really mind. He wasn't tired; he was still wondering at all of the things around him. It was nearly morning, though it was still extremely dark, before they reached firm ground. It was hard and dry, but Jasper was happy to be out of the mud. He couldn't have taken any more mud. It was wet, cold, and dirty. He felt like a butterfly emerging from a long sleep in a cocoon when he emerged from the mud, soaked and covered in the substance. They had come up behind another bunker, this one more stone and concrete than simply concrete. The group of them walked around the side of it silently, before one of the soldiers approached the entrance and whispered, "Flash!" There was a brief silence as the other soldiers held their rifles at the ready before, after a short pause, they heard someone whisper back, "Thunder!"

They entered the bunker on the alert, and then relaxed upon seeing friendly soldiers. "We thought we'd never find you, Mel." Jasper sat down against one of the bunker walls, following the lead of the other soldiers who did the same. The man in charge took Mel outside to discuss matters while the rest of the soldiers sat in the bunker and relaxed, if only for a brief moment.

"Man...I can't believe we've made it this far." The soldiers began talking between themselves. After what felt like several minutes, Jasper piped up, "What are we doing here?" The other soldiers stopped dead and stared at him. He stared back for a second before answering. "I need to know, what am I doing here?" Some of them looked down at the ground.

"Jasper," an older looking man started, "none of us want to be here. You know that. We don't even know why we're here, we can only guess. And that's it. We move on and forget about why we're fighting, and we just...*fight*."

Jasper was dissatisfied. "That's it?" he asked. "Can't somebody tell me what I'm doing here?"

Another younger soldier looked up from the ground and said, "Maybe you need to find that out for yourself, Jasper. You need to find out what you're fighting for. Me? I'm fightin' for my family, so they never have to be subjected to atrocities like this war. Find out what *you're* fighting for."

The bunker darkened and all of the other soldiers looked down at the ground. A single spotlight was drawn upon Jasper, then another lit up as Mel entered the room. Jasper could hear once more the Cellos plucking a low note. "Jasper," Mel said, "come with me." The young soldier looked up at Jasper and a spotlight lit upon him as well. "Remember," he said, "find out what you're fighting for." He looked down at the ground once more and the spotlight that had been on him disappeared. Jasper could hear the drum beginning to beat softy as he stood up and walked outside.

The fog had lifted, now, and the sky was dark and cloudy. It was, in fact, rather harsh looking. It was, Jasper thought, as if the sky was about to erupt and start pouring on them with much lightning. There was, however, a small area that allowed some light through, which he could see as rays pointing down to the earth from the skies. He looked at Mel, who was standing in front of a pile of boxes. As he moved closer, he noticed that, upon the pile of boxes, lay a map marked beyond belief with strategic plans drawn on it.

Mel spoke. "Jasper, we need you to take these men to an internment camp. There are a good number of prisoners there we believe."

Jasper was shocked. "I don't even know how I got here. You want me to lead the men?"

Mel frowned at him. "Jasper," he said, "you're the only person left capable. We need you to do this."

Jasper frowned and took off his helmet. He threw it to the ground where it landed with a loud crack. "How am I supposed to lead these men? I don't know where I am, I don't know how I got here, I don't know why I'm here! Hell, I don't even know who I am anymore!"

Mel scowled, but took a firm stand. He looked down at Jasper when he spoke. "Jasper, I wouldn't send you if I didn't have to, but you need to go to that internment camp. Don't you care about them?"

Jasper was stunned. "I don't even know them!"

With that comment, Mel stepped forward and grabbed Jasper by the jacket and pushed him up against the wall of the bunker. "It doesn't matter if you don't know them! We're all human! It doesn't matter who they are, where they came from, or what kind of people they are! If they don't help you that's their wrong, but if you don't help them, it's yours!" Mel was now screaming in his face and pushing him up against the stone bunker. "I need you to learn here, Jasper, and I need you to do it quick! What else do you have if you don't help these people? If you die, what do you take with you? Do you take your Goddamn money?!" He was firing saliva into Jasper's face, and he reminded Jasper of a bulldog barking viciously at potential prey.

He frightened Jasper, and his heart now pounded—after all, Mel was a bulldog with no leash.

"What have you gained by not helping them?!" He screamed.

Jasper pushed Mel back hard, and he nearly toppled over the stacked crates where the map rested. "I'll be alive, damn it!" he yelled back.

Mel breathed heavily and sat down on the ground, calming himself. From behind, Jasper heard a voice. "What have you got to judge life by without your deeds?" He looked back to see the young soldier standing there, in the spotlight once more. "It's all relative, man. How can you valuate life without having experienced death?" Jasper gasped for air now, too, and he breathed heavily.

He saw the whole lot of them standing there, inside the bunker, watching him from inside. Some of them looked appalled at his outburst, but their faces also showed understanding. They were all in the same boat, so to speak, and he knew that they all had, at one time or another, felt the same as he did. They all bore calm and slack faces, however tired by lack of rest, and their eyes were all locked on him.

A bulky soldier walked forward and put his hands on Jasper's soldier. "It's ok," he said almost sarcastically, "we trust you with our lives. Let's get moving." He walked back a few steps into the bunker, and all the other soldiers stood up from their places and stepped forward as well, carrying their rifles and packs with them. "Here," Mel said, "take this and get moving." Mel handed him the map, with his orders highlighted, and a sandwich. Mel gave Jasper another stern look before walking off around the bunker.

Standing now outside the bunker, Jasper noticed that there was nothing else around. He stood up on a crate and looked around, now that the fog had lifted, and observed the landscape. The other soldiers stood lower on the ground, staring up at him with odd looks on their faces while he did this. The field was entirely grass. Not long grass, but short, soft blades like that of a mowed lawn. It was dark in color and slightly grey. There was not a significant amount of color anywhere, actually, though Jasper had not taken note of this before. He looked down and noticed the faces staring at him with puzzled looks. Mel was nowhere to be seen now, not off in the distance nor anywhere nearby. Jasper stepped down from the pedestal on which he had been standing. He was growing to accept the situation he was now in, and he was glad that he would at least be free of the mud. "Alright," he said, "let's go."

Jasper felt scared and confused, as if he were lost in a dark forest at night time. He was tired and hungry, and sore everywhere, but he knew he had no choice but to soldier on. He started to walk off through the grass, followed closely by the other soldiers.

CHAPTER THREE

Battle Wounds

Jasper walked for many hours through the soft grass, five soldiers in tow. He had come to the conclusion that it would be best for him not to contest them; they were his only route to understanding his predicament, and he had become aware of that. Jasper had also realized that, apart from fighting, war was simply walking. Walk here, walk there. Run, then walk. Run, walk, hide, dive for cover. It was, to put it simply, just movement. It was like normal life, except more like living in a jungle where you were constantly watching for those who were hunting you. He asked himself several questions as a way of passing the time, and this was what had initially led him to this conclusion.

"What separates it from normal life?" He asked himself. You didn't have a permanent dwelling. It was more...*natural.* The thought that it was closer to nature initially appalled him, but he then found shelter from that feeling in that justification. It was, after all, true. War, he thought, is more like what we would have encountered if the world had not become 'civilized' as it is now. 'Civilization,' he concluded, was just life in nature without the hunting, or being hunted, and with much less walking.

Jasper used to go for long walks when he was a child, but it had been many years since he had done that and now his legs grew tired. Twice, he attempted to sit down for a rest, but as he was the leader and none of the other soldiers seemed to tire, he pushed himself onwards, trying very hard not to show his exhaustion to his comrades. He enjoyed walking, though he was just not capable of walking as long as he used to. The smoke that now clogged his lungs caused him to cough often. It was odd, he thought, that he had chosen to smoke. He had never particularly liked the smell of it before he started and, in all honesty, he didn't like it that much now. He was stifling himself, filling his own lungs with chemicals. Never before had he thought of it that way; it was just…*smoking.* That was it, until this moment. It was a choice, he realized. If it wasn't a choice he had now, because of his addiction, it was certainly a choice he had when he first tried smoking, the same choice that now condemned his lungs to light up like fire now, so many years later. He longed for a cigarette, a single stick, to help him numb out the pain of his life like the merciless snuffing of a candle.

Jasper reached up and felt his face. It was rough and unshaven, and it did not feel quite like he remembered it feeling. It felt…*older.* He had somehow aged several years already on this journey. He did not know how it was possible, but he knew that aging was, at least in real life, unavoidable. Perhaps he would grow old and then he would die, and that would be the end of his journey here. He hoped very much such was the case, because looking down at his larger and now

25

slightly wrinkled hands, he figured it would not be more than a few days before he died.

In this respect, Jasper had suddenly become aware of the fact that he was looking forward to death. An odd thing, he thought, something that was not particularly respected in the world to which he had become accustomed. Death, he thought, was something that was always rather feared. It was as if everybody assumed it was a bad thing. Even those who believed in heaven feared death, because they were afraid of hell. Jasper had never believed in hell, nor had he believed in heaven. He didn't know if there was a God or not, either, but he didn't care; he had just assumed that, when the time came, he would find out how things really worked. What had he to lose? Everybody died, he knew, and so he knew better than to worry about the inevitable and to just enjoy the time he was given.

"Get down!" someone whispered harshly. Jasper felt his knees collapse beneath him as he fell to the ground, face forward, startled by the sudden disappearance of his comrades who had all driven their bodies down to the ground faster than he had. Lying now in the grass, they saw a dark mobile unit similar to the one they had encountered in the mud, now approaching them. "Get ready!" he heard. He knew he was in charge and was the one who should be giving orders, though he also knew the other soldiers were aware of his predicament—he was not a soldier and, though he had fired a rifle before, he had never been a good leader. One short, almost stubby, soldier took

26

charge of the men, giving orders to everyone, and Jasper was grateful for it.

What was the meaning of this? Jasper could not bear it. Was this what it meant to be human? To fight and to kill and to torture? He could not believe that. His mind would not allow him such an easy reprieve. He laid his rifle down on the grass. Jasper looked down now, and saw that his uniform was bloodstained, though he knew it was not his blood. He rolled back onto his stomach and waited. He was exhausted and he breathed heavily. *What I would give*, he thought, *for a nice soft pillow right now.* Still, his thoughts bothered him with questions. What purpose did this serve? It was a question he assumed every soldier asked himself at one time or another. Surely, he thought, there had to be more to it than this. Life couldn't be just about getting ahead of each other. He waited for the enemy vehicle to approach.

Enemy, he contemplated. *Who is the enemy?* Certainly not them. From the perspective of the other side, though, perhaps they were indeed the enemy. It was all a matter of perspective, he thought. The opposition fought hard and long, so they must think that their purpose was for the best. Who had the authority to decide what was right, and what was wrong? *Simply because they think something is right,* he thought, *that didn't make it right, did it?* This boggled him, though he did not have time to dwell on it.

27

They heard the low rumbling of a truck coming up. Through the grass he could see almost nothing, just a lump of grey approaching. Jasper could hear laughing—there were two creatures sitting on top of the truck who were laughing and talking as they rode through the field. Their guns were slack and their faces were unsuspecting of their enemies lying in the grass. He lay there in wait, quietly. The stubby one looked over at him. "Jasper," he whispered harshly, "take the left side when it comes around. We have to take this one out. They aren't on our side." Jasper nodded, though he was frightened.

The engine continued toward them through the field, closer and closer, until it was nearly right on top of the soldiers. The one who had taken charge yelled, "Now!" and the five men began to fire from the grass, filling the enemies with holes. The ones on top fell off the roof to the ground where they moaned, until they were finished off by Jasper and another tall, lanky soldier. The driver took a shot to the head, which went through the glass and reddened the inside of the cab.

Three or four came out of the back of the supply truck, weapons firing, and Jasper instinctively shot the one who ran around the left towards him. He raised his rifle and took aim at the faceless head of his enemy, who was now firing wildly, and squeezed the trigger. The bullet opened the side of his enemy's head, though it was not a square hit. Cautiously, he walked around the side of the truck while the others walked to the right.

28

Jasper stood horrified, looking into the eyes of the now dead soldier who looked back up at him as he approached him. He thought they were fighting the creatures with no faces, and he had recognized no face from the distance, which he took the shot from. Instead, he found a normal human face staring up at him. Those eyes, he thought, that were full of life just seconds before. The eyes, now wide open, were peering through his soul, he felt. He could not bear to look at them any longer, and he kicked the soldier away and marched off to the front of the truck. A hand reached out and grabbed his foot as he turned. Looking down, the soldier who had been dead only a second ago was blinking and looking up at him, a whole in the side of his head. "Jasper!" he said quietly, "I'm going back where I came from!" Jasper pulled his leg free of the tight grip of his victim's hand. His heart was pumping, now, as he was shocked and frightened by the experience. His head felt like a balloon slowly filling with pressure.

The enemy who now lay on the ground looking quite pale and cold, still looked up at Jasper, though he spoke as if he felt no pain at all and moved as if he had suffered no injury. Jasper could hear the other soldiers walking at the back of the supply truck, and the man on the ground looked over before looking back at Jasper and speaking once more. "Remember," he said, his voice now dimming as he faded away, "we're all fighting for the same thing!" Jasper watched as the soldier went back to his former state of deadness before

29

looking up and peering around. He was unsure where the truck had come from, because there were no buildings in sight.

"Jasper, get your ass back here!" Jasper heard. Turning, he looked at the truck. He saw, now, that the other soldier had taken control entirely, which suited Jasper just fine. Smoke wafted from the pipe above the cab, and the lump now sat roasting in the sun like a piece of dead meat. He walked around the side to the back of the truck, where he met the other soldier standing, staring into the back of the truck. Inside the truck sat bags of food, a notebook from one of the deceased soldiers, and a small gold statue inlaid with diamonds and other colorful, precious stones.

Walking into the back, Jasper picked up the notebook. He also grabbed a ration from one of the bags, which he unpackaged and began to eat voraciously to help dull the pain of his empty stomach. Walking out the back, he sat down on the grass and opened the notebook. It was filled with poetry, and in the front was a photograph of the soldier he had killed sitting on a porch beside a woman. The first few pages were full of scribbled words and short phrases. Gnawing on a dehydrated carrot, which tasted nothing like an actual carrot, he flipped through the pages until he found something of interest. What he found was a short poem that stood out to him above the others.

A hot summer day, a snake in the grass,
I lie and wait for enemy brass,

And in the sun I ponder why,
Why do we fight, and why do we die?

And to my side my rifle lies,
Cold and dead, a lifeless mass,

And then, I hear it, at last!
Are those monsters here, I ask?

Then a rumble on the field,
Slowly up my comrades kneel,

Our rifles fire, a father screams,
The wounds inflicted never heal,

And yet they worsen still, the dreams,
The dreams of death and what it means,

And look into the dead man's eye,
One eye, not two, for one was gone,

I feel it when his children cry,
His curtains have been swiftly drawn,

And in the wake, what have I gained?
My eyes sunk low, my clothes all stained,

This war will be the end of me,
If not, my mind shall not agree,

And in the soil that soldier rests,
Passing now the final test,

I feel that he has damaged me,
More than I have damaged he,

For death is just a mystery,
Yet what we make is misery.

Jasper felt that the poem reflected his own experiences of war, and it struck him deeply. He voiced the words over and over in his mind, trying to understand the concept the deceased soldier tried to convey to him. He found it odd, also, that the scene described by the poem was so close to what he had just encountered. The soldier had, of course, not been missing an eye, but the similarity of the scene was nearly impeccable, apart from that discrepancy. It wasn't just the physical descriptions, but what and how he had felt only moments earlier.

Suddenly, Jasper heard another rumbling, this time different than what he had heard before. It was unlike anything he had ever experienced; he didn't just hear the rumbling, he felt it in his feet, which were not planted firmly on the ground. The ground shook and he could see the canvas of the back of the supply truck shaking.

As Jasper turned to face the truck and the other soldiers, he saw the one who had taken charge earlier holding the gold statue and another soldier scolding him. "It's got no value here, it will slow you down! Let it go!" Still, though, the soldier held onto the gold statue. It seemed that he was unaware of the rumbling, though the other soldiers were pulling at the one who argued. "Come on!" he said stubbornly, "we have to get out of here! You can't take it!" The stubby soldier stubbornly clutched the statue, which was a depiction of an elephant, by the trunk. The golden elephant looked quite heavy, and he made it only ten feet in thirty seconds or so. "Come on, Jasper!" the other soldiers screamed. Jasper stood up and dropped the notebook he had been holding, as well as the half eaten dehydrated carrot. He could feel the ground beating, and it was as if it were a heartbeat.

He slowly realized that the sound of a heartbeat he was hearing and feeling was a drum, and that there were other instruments playing a strong, loud piece as well. He saw the other soldiers take off, and he tried to catch up to them, though he could barely keep up. He heard marching, now, which matched the sound of the heartbeats. The ground was vibrating with such force that he could almost see the grass moving. Looking outwards, he saw the other soldiers running away. He turned around and looked back at the truck, where he saw the stubby soldier trying to catch up to him, dragging the gold statue behind him. He could see the source of the vibration, now, as well. He could see hundreds of thousands of soldiers closing in on them. Helicopters filled the sky, hundreds of them, and more soldiers dropped from them. He was now between the soldiers running away and the supply truck.

The supply truck seemed to be swallowed up by the enormous crowd of soldiers who were getting closer and closer. The soldier dragging the statue was now overrun, his figure disappearing into the ocean of militants who trampled his body into the ground. The other soldiers, who were still running, now ran back towards him as they were all completely surrounded. They neared him once more, but were also consumed by the crowd before they reached him. He stood in the center, completely surrounded, as he was stifled. When the soldiers were within few feet of him, he could see they all bore no faces. They all closed in on him, though several rushed ahead of the group that closed in on him, waiving heavy-looking black batons in the air. The instruments of the orchestra were now making a ghastly screeching noise, the drums beating now faster and out of tune, and, as Jasper's pursuers reached him, he crouched down on the ground and screamed "Heeeeelp!" before all went black. The last thing he could feel was his head colliding with a rather hard object, leaving the imprint of a dull beating sound on his mind as he fell face-first into the grass.

Chapter Four

The Dream

Though Jasper knew he was unconscious, he was still aware. He wasn't sure whether that meant he was conscious or not, though it didn't matter. He tried to stand up, but he eventually realized that he had no legs to walk with, nor did he have two arms with which to lift himself. In fact, he had none of the appendages with which he had become accustomed to using for mobility. Instead, he felt that he had something else. He had…antennae, and he became aware of multiple legs. He had no fingers, either. It was dark, and he could barely see. Exactly what was in front of him he did not know, but it was moveable. It was a stiff substance, slightly green, or at least that is what he could make out in the current light.

Jasper felt as if he was tied up by a rope, unable to move. He began to try to free himself, pushing and writhing. He did this for several minutes before, with one final push of two or three of his legs, he pushed a hole through the wall of his area of captivation. He pushed harder than he had ever pushed before, tearing and shoving his way through the side of what seemed to be his cocoon. He was blinded by the light for a second before he became aware of the fact that he was amongst beautiful flowers and plants, emerging from his prison which was adhered to the side of a rather large sunflower. The sun was warm, and the breeze dried his new wings quickly, which he spread open to reveal a brilliant array of colors. He began to flutter his wings and, soon, he was in the air.

"Where am I?" Jasper asked himself. "How did I get here?" He couldn't remember where he had come from, though the question was on his mind. He had just been thrown there, no memories of where he was prior to this time, and he was unaware of many things, one of them even being what he was. *What am I?* He did not know. Either way, he thought, it was a happy place to be. It was calm and he felt free. Free from stress, free from expectations, free from pain, free from suffering, and free from his addictions. Jasper grew to love flowers in a very short time and enjoyed life in the garden.

Jasper was fluttering around happily and contentedly in the world. Suddenly, a child with a net appeared in front of him, and he flew around the child's head. The child was holding a net, which oscillated in the air. A pair of almond shaped eyes, as cold as ice, yet as warm as the sun, chased Jasper, the butterfly, rapidly around the garden. The butterfly continued to rove the garden. Suddenly, the net came down towards him, missing very nearly. A red and yellow flower exploded into a cloud of petals and pollen as the net impacted it forcefully. The net whipped viciously back up through the air. Jasper fled, rising high above the child's head and away from the garden. From up so high he could see how expansive the world was. He saw a lake, a farm, and a large building off in the distance. The butterfly floated back down to the ground once more.

Suddenly, again the net came down and, with the strength of a God, the child pulled Jasper from the air. The Child grabbed him and placed him in a jar—one which housed many other butterflies. Jasper looked outside the jar, through the glass, which blurred his vision of the outside world. He felt so stifled, so contained. The other butterflies crowded him, interested to meet him. They eventually forgot about him, though, and he, like them, forgot about what was outside of the jar. In fact, he forgot that he was in the jar altogether. The jar was his home. He simply ate at the grass that had been placed in the jar and was completely content.

Then Jasper began to fly around the jar. "Why do I have these wings," Jasper asked himself, "if I have nowhere to fly?" Then he remembered the world beyond the glass walls of the jar, and he peered outside through the glass. It was blurry, but he could see! There was a world outside! Jasper began to flap his wings and fly around the jar hurriedly, smashing off the walls of the jar. "What are you doing?" the other butterflies asked, frightened of his actions. They kept their distance. "I am trying to free myself from this stifling prison!" Jasper yelled. The other butterflies shrugged and backed away.

Jasper soon became tired, though, and he fell to the bottom of the jar where he rested from his fight for freedom. The butterflies were consuming all of the air in the jar, and it had become more stifling and difficult to breathe. The sunlight heated the jar, and it became hot. Jasper couldn't live under these conditions for long—none of them could. Suddenly, through the jar the image of a large human foot became visible to the butterflies. The jar rose through the air. A great pair of hands removed the lid of the jar, and Jasper was free once more. "Come with me!" he shouted to the other butterflies. "We're free!" he screamed ecstatically. He flew up high to the warm blue sky.

The other butterflies did not follow, though. They stuck to their jar and refused to move. Jasper yelled to them, but they couldn't hear him, because he had distanced himself from them. He flew back towards the jar, but the child was holding the net and he feared being caught again. The others did not move. The child shook the jar viciously, holding it upside down, and some of the butterflies were forced out of the jar. Most of them, though, were too worn down to fly away, and their wings were shrunken and dried from spending too much time in the hot jar baking in the sun. Jasper flew above everything, up into the sky. He looked around and saw once more the expansive land from which he had come. "I'm alive!" he screamed, tears running down his face. He was so happy, happier than he had ever been before. "I'm alive!" he screamed again.

Jasper attempted to flap his wings and fly, but it was becoming hard. The sky turned red, and everything that surrounded him disappeared. The ground below seemed to grow away from him, expanding farther and farther downwards. He tried to flap his wings again. He couldn't, though, because he had none. Jasper was no butterfly. His descent grew faster and faster, and darker and darker, until he finally neared the bottom. He screamed as he plummeted toward the hard surface that now rose up to meet him. As he fell to the ground, he felt cold, and the hard surface turned to water. Jasper, falling head first, fell into the water and, as he made his final impact, he awoke with a start, sitting up briskly and breathing heavily. His face was sweaty, and he was shivering with cold. He leaned against the wall and covered his hands with his face.

CHAPTER FIVE

Captivated

The first thing Jasper was aware of when he awoke was his headache, which pierced his skull like a spear through a freshly picked pumpkin. It felt as if his head was exploding, and its contents were attempting to free themselves from the prison of his skull. If only they would escape, he thought, then maybe he too could escape his prison. At least, that was his hope. It was, he decided, his only chance of getting back to society—death, he thought, was his only shred of hope for getting back to where he had come from.

He felt his head ache with sharp pain, and he lifted his hands to his temples. He realized immediately after doing this that his hands were chained together, and that he was shackled to an old-looking stone wall. There was a single light bulb in his cell, which flickered occasionally, which was the only dim source of light. There was a heavy steel chain connecting his hands, which was then attached to the wall. His legs were held together by a chain of similar sorts, which was attached to a large, black, steel ball, which he assumed was intended to keep him in place. His movement was quite limited, and he leaned up against the damp and cracked brick wall behind him.

After several seconds of staring up at the ceiling, Jasper began to search for a way out. He discovered that his movement was quite limited—he could, in fact, move only a foot or less in either direction. The heavy steel ball attached to his feet was nearly too heavy to lift; in his current weakened state, he could barely move it out of his way by pushing on it with his foot and with his back against the wall—let alone lift it—and the only way he could see to get out of the shackles was with a key, as indicated by the keyhole located on each of the cuffs of his legs. His arms, he observed, were shackled together and then held to the wall by another chain with a separate lock; he could find no indication of a keyhole for the chains surrounding his wrists.

The cell he sat in was cold and dark, and he shivered. He could see his breath, which disappeared into the air shortly after appearing there whenever he exhaled. He struggled for a minute or so, pulling at his chains. To his right was another wall, and to his left were more sets of shackles, balls, chains, and other devious devices of captivity. In front of him was nothing; no bars, nothing. The light bulb hanging from a solitary wire on the ceiling dimmed and flickered, still. He could see that he was in a sort of basement, and around the corner to his right there was a set of stairs that he could barely see from where he sat. He began to thrash about with force, pulling and wrenching at his bonds until his wrists were red and bruised. His face became red, and his anger rose as he yelled and fussed over the bonds.

He had tired himself out before he sunk down to the ground, head resting down on his chest because it was the only semi-comfortable position he could achieve. He examined himself now, and he realized that he was battered and bruised. He also took notice of the fact that he was no longer wearing his military uniform; instead, he was wearing a jumpsuit similar to what a prisoner would wear. In fact, it was exactly what a prisoner would wear; it bore black and white horizontal stripes, like that of a zebra, and it was quite old and dirty. Sitting, now quietly, in his dark and cold cell, he became suddenly aware of a sound. Looking up briskly, he listened intently to the sound. It was…footsteps. He could hear the sharp thumping of marching, similar to what he had heard prior to being captured. Carefully, he tried to discern the source of the sound. It sounded to him as if the footsteps were approaching, and time proved him correct.

Within the short time span of about two minutes, the source of the footsteps came into clear view. Two faceless beasts who seemed to draw no breath at all dragged in one of his comrades and threw him down on the ground. Jasper backed off as much as he could, looking down at his comrade who looked beaten, sore, and tired. The soldiers who had marched in were followed closely by three more, one of whom carried a set of keys. Kneeling down, the beastly thing grabbed the soldier, who now looked nearly dead, and dragged him into place with immense strength. Forcing his arms and legs into the chains, the soldier was locked into place with little argument. The man was in no condition to object, anyway.

The five strange beings marched off up the stairs, and Jasper was left with his fellow soldier. It took him a second to recognize the man: he was the soldier who had instructed him to "find what he was fighting for," though his face was now almost unrecognizable for the cuts and bruises. He seemed to be barely conscious, and Jasper whispered to him. "Hey, are you alright?"

The soldier rolled over a bit before answering. "Yea, I think I'll be alright." His lips were dry and cracked and nearly blue. "What about you?"

Jasper was surprised at the soldier's consideration toward him. Apart from a splitting headache and deep hunger pains, he felt relatively fine. "I'm ok," Jasper replied.

The soldier looked around before spitting out a piece of wire he had been holding in his mouth. "I stuffed that in my mouth before they tied me up. Nearly swallowed it when they threw me down here."

Jasper smiled at the soldier's ingenuity. "Can you pick a lock?" Jasper shook his head. "Damn," the man retorted, "neither can I."

Jasper tried to reach the piece of wire that lay only an inch out of his reach. "Could you?" he asked. The man next to him flicked it towards him and he picked it up, and began trying at the lock bands that attached his handcuffs to the wall.

The soldier, watching, spoke freely to Jasper while he worked at his lock with the wire. "You know," he started, "I never believed in this war. Not until I

43

started fighting it." Jasper feigned interest as he worked away, looking back and forth between the lock and the soldier's bruised and bleeding face. He looked relaxed, Jasper thought. "And then…I realized. We all have to fight, or we never move ahead." Jasper slowed his work on the lock for a moment as he listened, now a little more interested. The man continued. "I used to think that I could just avoid the fight, you know? Just…stay at home, while the soldiers fought. And then I was forced into it, and I finally understand it. I get, now, why people *choose* to fight." Jasper continued to work on his lock again while he listened, now nearly getting his lock undone. "And now that I've fought my battle, I've made it to the end. I've learned what I needed to learn, and that's it."

Jasper stopped and looked up into the man's eyes. "Don't say that. We'll get out of here." The man looked down at the ground for a moment, then looked back up at Jasper. "No…you will, but I think I'm through. I've learned what I came here to learn, and now I'm heading back to where I came from. I think, though, that you will be here for some time more." Jasper was about to scold the man for talking that way before he realized that death, here, was his ultimate goal as well. It was not a bad thing for the man to die, it was just another phase. It was a phase of life that even he would have to experience both here and in reality, or at least where he thought reality was.

"Jasper…listen. I've been here before. I've been in a place like this." Jasper still stared silently. "Then they came for us. I escaped, but the man next to me wasn't as fortunate. It was all just luck, I suppose, that I was able to crack my lock open against the wall." He indicated the lock Jasper was trying to open. "They'll try to keep you, Jasper. They'll want you to be like them, but don't listen. It's how you become like them, like everyone else here. Be different."

Jasper picked at his lock with his wire, and his lock cracked open. He had discovered how to open the locks, and he began to do the same on the shackles around his feet. "So is this it?" he asked, while he worked. "You just accept it, and I leave you here?"

The beaten soldier gave a faint smile. "Yes, something like that."

Jasper's feet became free of the heavy steel ball first, then free of each of the bands around his feet. He stood up and walked over to the stairs, looking up the hallway only a few feet above his head, up the short staircase. He peered back at the soldier once more, who waved a chained hand at him, indicating that he should leave. He took a few steps up the stairs. His heart was thumping and his knees were shaking. His teeth chattered from the combination of fear and cold that now filled him, and he slid along the wall up the staircase, afraid of what he might find.

At the top of the staircase, he saw that the old stone walls ended and that an expansive hall of prison cells began. Row by row he passed them by slowly, walking between them. Some eyes followed him, and soon the cell's inhabitants began to stand and walk to the front of their cells. Their bony arms and hands stuck out through the bars into the hallway, which was quite narrow, and grabbed at him as he walked by. At first they said nothing, but soon they began to beg him to stay. "Stay with us!" they said. "Don't leave us here! Come be with us!" He turned around at the first hand that grabbed his shoulder, frightened by it, and fell over onto the ground, tripping over his own feet. The hands grabbed at him more viciously as he crawled back from them, only to meet more. The hallway was long. Soon they were yelling at him, shouting and screaming for him to stay with them. "Stay," they cried, "don't leave us! Be with us!"

He knew he could not free them, and he knew that they were aware of that also. Neither did he think it was wise to stay with them; why would he stay there when he could be free? They wouldn't like it, but he knew he had to free himself. Throwing himself forward, he scrambled along the floor of the hallways on all fours. The hallway was lit also by the dim light bulbs hanging from the ceiling, which cast dark and scary shadows among the halls. The rotting, bony, and leprous hands grabbed at his clothes as he continued along the floor. He got up onto his knees, and then up onto his feet. He moved quickly through the hall, now sweating heavily from fear and exhaustion. "No!" he yelled, "No! Let me out! Let me go! I need to get out!" he screamed continuously.

One grabbed him with an intensely strong grip, which forced him to turn and look into the horrible

46

face, which seemed to be rotting away. It was as if all of the facial features had been slowly disappearing, eaten away by a disease. It was like leprosy, and the man he saw was already missing most of his facial features, which left behind an almost entirely blank slate adhered to the front side of his head. Jasper let out a scream upon seeing this and turned around and ran down the hallway. It seemed forever as he ran, hands brushing along his clothes and attempting to grab him and hold him back with them as he went. "Let me out!" he screamed. "LET ME OUT!" he repeated. He said it three or four times before he finally reached the end of the hallway. The hallway had now erupted into a wild mishmash of yelling, grasping, and clutching. The noise, he knew, would draw attention. He stood still for a moment, kneeling to catch his breath and looking once more down the hallway before continuing.

Upon exiting, he came upon a small office full of old wooden furniture. The room resembled his basement cell where his comrade now sat alone, except for the few furnishings, such as the desk and closet that designated it as an office. The lighting in there was seemingly as poor as it was everywhere else, and like the cell, it gave him the feeling that he was underground. He could hear running, though it was in tune like marching. There were several men, or whatever they were, approaching the office. He looked out the other entrance to the office, which, similar to the entrance he had come through, bore no door. He could see several figures coming toward the office.

Hurriedly, he ran back toward the closet and opened it. Jasper quickly thrust himself inside, among several uniforms and jackets, and closed the door briskly but silently. He was careful to make no noise when closing the door.

He could hear the noise of marching approaching. They continued until they were directly in front of the closet before stopping, and then he heard voices. "You two, go down and retrieve the two from the basement cell while we quiet down these noisy prisoners." After he had heard the figures move away from the closet and down the hallway with the cells, he opened the closet door and looked around the corner to see that there were soldiers marching down toward the cell where he had been. The others were going from cell to cell quieting down the prisoners. One looked back, and Jasper pulled his head away from the corner. He stayed quietly, clenching his fists and holding his eyes closed, hoping that he had not been spotted. He waited for nearly a minute before returning to the corner to see two soldiers rushing up the hallway, one dragging his comrade along with him.

Jasper saw the other being, bearing no face and wearing a grey uniform, running up toward another. Something was spoken hurriedly and seriously, and Jasper decided that it was time for him to leave. He ran through the office and through the other doorframe, rushing down that hallway. He entered a large room, again, similar to the others, which contained only a wooden table and a large steel door. He heard footsteps rushing towards him, and so he pushed on the heavy door. It was difficult to open, but with much force, he quickly had opened it and he crawled through, pushing it closed behind him with both hands once he was on the other side.

Upon exiting the complex, Jasper immediately observed the prison yard he was now standing in. There were large concrete walls that surrounded the main building, and there were several holdings such as the one he had just exited scattered among the prison yard. He could see an enormous steel gate, which equated to the size of a fairly large building. The walls were extremely high, and there were guard towers with large spotlights in each of them, which made spots of light prowl the ground both for intruders and for escapees, such as Jasper. He crawled along the side of the wall for a short ways. He heard a sound behind him and immediately fell to the ground, lying in the grass. He could see the large steel door open with great ease, and then four of the odd creatures emerged from it. He could hear them squabbling for a moment, probably over his escape, and then he watched them run off toward a large grey brick building, which stood at the center of the yard.

He stood up and began to slink through the yard, weaving in and out of dark and light spots and doing his best to avoid the spotlights, which avidly searched for him. Suddenly, he heard a loud horn begin to howl like a wolf. It was enormously loud, and he knew it would mean no good. There were horns placed upon dilapidated telephone poles with no wires all around the complex, and he could hear the siren blowing louder and louder each time he approached one of the poles. He heard the sound of a large gate opening and, peering around the side of one of the prison cell complexes, he could see a large steel gate drawing upwards, revealing a door through which three large dogs emerged.

The dogs were not normal dogs—nothing in this place seemed normal to him, though it did to its regular inhabitants he assured himself—and he could barely make out their oddities and distortions from such a distance. He could see that, unlike a normal dog, these dogs bore extremely long and sharp teeth, which extended from the top down to where their chins should be. The thought of meeting one of those dogs face to face frightened him, and he ran from them. The sirens continued to blow as he crawled amongst the prison complex, searching frantically for an exit. "Come on!" he told himself, "there has to be a way out of here." He continued, now fearing the dogs more, which were prowling the grounds for him.

Suddenly, Jasper quickly turned a corner around the side of a small building and found himself face to face with one of the beasts. It had no eyes, only sockets where eyes should have been. The beast's fur was mangled and dirty, and it's teeth, no matter how sharp and frightening, were slightly yellow and rotting. The first thing he noticed about the thing was it's smell, which he actually noticed before seeing the beast itself.

It stood at about breast level to him. He started to back off slowly, and it began to growl and snarl.

He began to back away now, faster, and the beast began to bark as he turned his back towards it and ran. He ran for his life, faster and faster. He knew he couldn't outrun the beast, which was now nearly nipping at his heels with its ferocious looking teeth. His lungs burned, but he ignored it and ran. His heart beat faster and faster, and louder and louder, until he could feel it clearly beating throughout his body. The other two dogs were running across the field toward him, and the guards were running also, following closely behind the vicious dog-like creatures despite their speed.

Jasper suddenly spotted a large crack in one of the great concrete walls of the prison complex, and he ran towards it, barely keeping ahead of his angry pursuers. The spotlights, now, were on him and the dog. There were several of them, which blinded him and kept him illuminated for all to see. It was something he feared, being seen. If he could just slink away and hide, not letting his presence be known, he would be happy. Instead, though, he had found himself in this unavoidable predicament.

His lungs continued to drag him down, wearing on him like a file on a piece of soft wood. His tired legs could barely drag him any farther. His knees shook and his body and his strength seemed to fade and fail him. He was beginning to slump, though he was nearing the crack in the wall. The crack extended from near the top, right down to the bottom, where there was a hole just large enough for a small person to fit through. The problem that Jasper had to face now was that he was not a small person; or at least he was full grown and looked to be too large to fit through. There were now several guards and all three dogs pursuing him, and he reached the crack just as one of the dogs came close to pulling on his striped outfit.

He took a dive towards the hole, his only chance to make it, and he slid through. He could feel his sides scraping against the rough concrete as he went, and he almost didn't make it. As he pulled himself through the hole, he felt a tug on his suit. He tried to pull away, but it pulled at him with such an immense strength that he could not. Turning, now, he put one foot on the wall and pulled with all of his strength, watching as he was slowly pulled back towards the hole by his pant leg, held by the teeth of one of the ferocious dog creatures. He pulled with all of his strength, and the dog seemed to drag him back effortlessly, until, finally, the teeth that tugged at the cuff of his pants ripped through the material and tore a piece off, letting him go.

He pulled himself away from the hole with his hands, watching, frightened, as one of the dog creatures attempted to fit through the hole. It was, fortunately for Jasper, too large, and the last thing he could see of it was it's snarling eyeless face growling at him before it pulled back into the hole. Jasper stood up, tired, and leaned over to catch his breath. He dared not slow, though, because he knew that they would pursue him;

his captors would want him to stay there, and become like them at any cost. He couldn't afford to become like them, to lose his facial features and everything he stood for. He couldn't just...*assimilate.* He picked up a jogging pace, and the sound of sirens and barking dog creatures faded behind him as he distanced himself from the prison yard, jogging off tiredly through the thick fog that now blanketed the field ahead of him.

CHAPTER SIX

Simply Floating

Jasper walked through the thick fog, barely able to see in front of him. He had not realized until after exiting the prison yard that he was still shackled around his wrists and, though his hands were now more free than before, he was still not completely free of his bonds. As he walked for many hours, the chains became heavier and heavier, and he became more tired; the steel bonds began to cut into his wrists as they rubbed on his skin. He had escaped his captors, but he knew that it wasn't over; after all, if it were, he was sure that he would not be there trekking through the thick fog.

The grass beneath his feet was soaked with dew, and it was beginning to lighten outside. It was still dark out, darker than it had been earlier, but he knew the dawn was approaching. "Perhaps," he thought, "I will be able to see once the fog is gone." He continued to walk onward, toward his ultimate destination, though he did not know what that destination was.

He heard a sound, then, as he walked on through the fog. It was the sound of water. Not rushing water, but calm water, which moved only with slight waves. He could not see where it was coming from through the fog, so he headed toward the sound. He was at first wary and questioned whether or not to approach it, but he then came to the conclusion that there could be nothing worse in this place than where he had just come from.

As he approached the sound, he saw a shape in the distance through the fog. Picking up his speed, he tiredly jogged toward it. It was only a short while before an old wooden dock came into view, as well as the source of the sound, which was a network of water-filled canals that weaved in and out of several old wooden buildings. He realized that the canals were not, actually, canals, but rather roadways of water that flowed down between the wooden buildings, which were afloat on the water. The dock was nearly falling apart, and the posts to which it was held were sticking diagonally out of the water which, too, were partially obscured by the fog. The air smelled of salt and fish and, though the thought of eating fish was not particularly appetizing at that moment, he decidedly would have eaten anything because of the hunger that now pained his stomach.

He climbed up onto the dock and then across a wooden board onto a walkway around one of the wooden buildings. He saw no people, though he figured that the buildings must have been owned by someone. Continuing around the building, he saw a sidewalk of wooden boards ejected from the side of one of the buildings. There were also several small wooden bridges that hung down nearly to the water between the buildings. It seemed to be a whole town, or even a city, floating on the water. After several minutes of walking around carefully, he reached an edge of the town on the side opposite where he had entered.

Jasper could see the sun now, cutting it's way through the fog. It was rising shallowly in the distance, though it was still dark. In the sky he saw the most beautiful arrangement of stars he had ever seen before. When he was a child, the stars were brilliant, but they bore no comparison to those he could now see in the sky with such amazing clarity. He felt as if he could reach out and touch them. There were nebulas, and stars, and even planets, which were closer than the moon had been to earth. He could see, also, more than one sun; he could see several, actually. There were also several moons, similar to the moons of Earth, and he could see more than just red in the sky. He could see blues and greens, reds and yellows, and more. He could see colors that he had never seen before, which baffled him. He felt as if he was looking into his own soul, staring up at the sky now, which warmed the inside of him for a brief moment. He knew that it would be too bright to see the stars momentarily, so he stared at them for as long as he could.

Jasper came back to his body after a short while and continued to wander the town. "Hello!" he called, hoping to hear a friendly voice in response. Much to his surprise, he did. "Hello!" he heard returned. He rushed quickly around several buildings, up and down the sidewalks and across bridges until he came to the other side of the small floating village.

Upon reaching the other side, Jasper came across a rather old man sitting in a chair smoking a large cigar. The man wore a captain's hat and looked as if he had not shaved in several days. His eyes were grey, and they sunk low into his head. "Good morning," the man said, "The name's William. You can call me Bill." He extended his hand, which was missing two fingers. Though Jasper was perturbed by this, he shook the man's hand anyway. "Welcome to my home."

Jasper was happy to have found a welcoming face. The man smiled. "Where am I?" Jasper asked.

"I don't know, to be honest. I don't think anybody knows where we are." The man stood up from his rocking chair with great difficulty and grabbed a short, wooden cane with an eagle's head at one end and a sharp brass spike at the other. He used the cane to walk. "Come on," he said, "We'll talk inside. You look hungry." Jasper followed him instinctively.

The two of them walked around the corner and went into a wooden building. It was warm inside, though Jasper did not know how since everything appeared to be made of long poles of wood—the light of outside now poured through the cracks on the side and back walls. There was a lit candle on one of the tables, which rocked back and forth as they moved with the waves. Jasper thought it unwise to have a candle rocking inside of a wooden building while they weren't there, but Bill showed no concern. Bill walked over to a cupboard and removed a bag, and then walked over to the table near the door which Jasper was standing beside. "Sit, son, sit," he said. Jasper took a seat. Bill removed a piece of bread and a small lump of smoked fish from the heavy cloth bag, wrapped in what appeared to be dried seaweed. "Here," he said, "eat this. It's not the greatest, but it'll get you through the day." Jasper took it and thanked him, wolfing it down greedily. "Would you like water?" Bill asked. "It's the one thing we have plenty of." Jasper said no because, though his mouth was dry and his lips were cracked, he was afraid of what might be in the water.

After Jasper had finished eating the bread and fish, Bill began to talk. "Now," he said, "you look a bit concerned. Not to mention the fact that you're bleeding, wearing a prisoners outfit, and your hands are chained." He smiled, and Jasper gave a chuckle.

"I don't know where I am, and I have no idea how I got here." The man laughed. "You said that," he said with a smile. "We're all in the same boat." Jasper ignored the pun. "Nobody here knows how they got here. Nobody here knows where we came from. And, more than that, we don't even know where we're headed!"

Jasper smiled again. He felt the same way, and he knew that he was indeed in the same boat, though he knew where he wanted to go. The only problem was getting there. "I want to get back to where I came from," Jasper said, "and I don't know how to do that."

The sailor looked at him for a moment before answering. "I'm as lost as you, Jasper. Always have been. I never really had any guidance, nobody to tell me where to go. So I've just been floating around here on this vessel trying to figure out where I'm headed."

Jasper stared at him. "Where can I go?" he asked.

Bill smiled. "Nowhere to go but forwards. I can take you across if you want. There isn't much more on this side of the lake." Jasper had nearly forgotten that he was on a large floating village, though he still rocked back and forth with the waves.

"I've got nowhere else to go," Jasper said, "so I'd love it if you could give me a lift. I'm sorry, but I've got nothing to offer as pay, though."

The man laughed heftily before giving his reply. "Don't worry about it, there's no money in this place anyway." Jasper smiled and thanked him.

"By the way," Jasper asked, "what is this place?"

He was met with a proud and strong reply. "This," Bill said, "is the Sailing Vessel San Maria, the finest vessel on this lake." Jasper was a little displeased with the vague answer, but he didn't want to ask more of the man. "I'll go untie us and draw up the anchor," Bill said, "I'll be back in a few minutes and we'll get going. There's a bed upstairs, there's one in every building here, so feel free to have a rest if you need. You look like crap." Jasper smiled and thanked him once more. Though he had originally planned on denying that offer, when Bill left, he went up the rickety wooden stairs and fell asleep on the "bed."

It was several hours before Jasper was awakened by the surprise of a large drop of water falling between his eyes and splashing on his face. He was expecting to find himself lying in bed at his old apartment, but instead he awoke and found that he was lying on a pile of straw—what Bill had called a bed—and that he was wet. It was drizzling rain now, and it was cold. He could see his breath, and he could feel the water dripping down on him from the spaces between each roof pole. He lay still on the pile of straw, in his dirty striped uniform. Slowly, Jasper sat up. He was stiff and his bruises hurt. His comrade had not been lying to him; he literally was fighting. He was struggling with the task of breaking free from the binds that now held him, and he was struggling with himself. He curled up in the corner for a moment and quietly cried to himself, sick of the place he was in. He longed to escape and to go back where he had come from, but he just hadn't made it there yet. He assured himself that he would make it back before he wiped his face and went down the stairs.

Jasper could see Bill through the spaces in the back wall—he was sitting in his rocking chair, wearing his captain's hat and smoking—and he exited through the door. He walked around the side of the building and approached Bill, who looked up at him. Bill spoke before he had did. "You know, we're all just floating out here. We're just floating." Jasper felt odd suddenly, provoked by the awkward conversation Bill had started.

Bill continued. "We're just…we've all just been sent here without explanation. We've been put here without reason, and we haven't even been told what we've got to do. We're all just out here on our own boats floating around aimlessly."

Jasper continued to listen, now not daring to speak.

"I'm happy, though. I'm happy, mate. I'm content to just…float. I'm alright with it here; it's what I know. I like it."

"Are you really happy, William?" Jasper asked, hoping to provoke him to expand a little with a question. Bill looked over at him, his sunken eyes leering into Jasper's. "Yes," he said flatly and insistently, "I'm happy." Jasper had obviously struck a nerve, and Bill ended the topic there.

"We're almost there," he said. "You can see the other side." He pointed to the land that was now relatively close to them. "We should be there in less than two minutes." Jasper took a few steps closer and sat on the edge of the sidewalk. There was a large, dead fish hanging from a large wooden winch by the edge of the water near where he had sat down, and he could smell it. Jasper turned around and spoke to Bill once more as they approached the other shore. "Thank you, Bill. Thank you for everything. I wouldn't have made it across without you."

Bill smiled. "That's what I'm here for, son. I don't know what I'd do if the lake up and vanished. I'd have no more passengers."

"That's another thing I meant to ask you about," Jasper began, "where are all the passengers? This vessel seems a bit large for just you."

Bill looked down at the ground. He seemed to be sad, now, and Jasper could see his eyes nearly welling up with tears. A single violin played quietly, which Jasper could hear. He had forgotten all about the audience and the orchestra. He could now hear that the orchestra was still looming invisibly about the scene, but the faces of the audience were gone for the moment from Jasper's vision. Bill looked up and wiped his eyes with his sleeve, sniffling. "They get fewer every year. A few hundred years ago, this ship was entirely full. They've disappeared, my passengers. I used to have to fill all of the rooms and catch more fish." He indicated a row of fish winches farther along the side where no fish hung. "Now I catch one fish and I smoke and dry as much as I can, but I end up throwing it out to the water. It seems there are fewer people taking this journey now than ever. I won't lie, it makes me sad, Jasper." Jasper was unsure how Bill had known his name—he couldn't remember telling him, at least.

Bill continued. "And I'll tell you what, Jasper, nobody can force them to come, so they don't come. It's a sea they dare not brave, if you catch my drift." The violin became stronger and more powerful as Bill's voice grew with it. "Can they not see it, Jasper? If none ventured here, this place would die! It's getting close, now. I'm sure you saw that disgusting prison yard. Things are falling apart here, Jasper."

Jasper became intrigued, now, to know more about the place where he was. "What do you mean?" Jasper asked.

"This place, this whole world, Jasper," Bill replied, "It's dying! The crowds of people aren't coming any more. The war is consuming everything there is, and those faceless bastards are destroying everything in their path!"

Bill now raged onwards, the intensity of his voice growing to the point where he was almost yelling with a sad fury. "The people who used to come here, it used to be so grand! The buildings crumble here now, even the very people seem to rot! Everything is dying!" The violin screamed as Jasper heard the bow draw across the strings furiously. "They're like a tornado, sucking everything in their path! They force everyone to conform, and then there's nothing left! Nobody comes here because they know that the tornado wants to suck them in if they don't conform!" The violin was joined by several other instruments, all intensely playing the loudest and strongest music Jasper had ever heard. Bill now yelled at the top of his lungs. "And they don't realize that they're adding to the goddamn tornado by not coming here and by not going against it! They don't realize that they've already been sucked in!" He came to a sudden stop with the last sentence, which was screamed at the top of his lungs. The instruments slowed down and the song returned to it's prior slow, sad state. There was now only a single violin playing.

"And…there's nothing we can do, Jasper." The impact of the silence and the final words of Bill's speech hit Jasper hard.

"There must be something…" Jasper said quietly.

Bill gave him a stern look, staring deeply into his pupils. "All we can do is go the journey ourselves and hope that they follow our lead. Your lead, Jasper."

Jasper understood, now, part of his purpose, though he did not understand all of it. Looking down, he wondered how he would get his hands unshackled. Or if he would. The captain, he thought, had not entirely freed himself of his own shackles, though he had at least made it this far.

They approached the other shore, and Jasper stood up on the walkway while they pulled up closely to an old wooden dock, nearly identical to the one on the opposite side of the lake. "How can you tell what side of the lake you're on?" he asked Bill, as he jumped down onto the shore. The two sides seemed to be almost identical. Bill chuckled as he pushed against the shore, heading back to the other side. He called back to Jasper. "It's easy, son! You can see clearly, there's no fog over here!" Jasper smiled and waved with both hands, because his hands were still chained, and he walked onwards, noticing that he could indeed see clearly—there was no fog on this side at all.

CHAPTER SEVEN

The Fog Lifts

Jasper could see clearly, now, though there was not much to see. Off in the distance he could see mountains. There was nothing much, really, just dry and cracked desert ground. It was not hot, much like a desert, but had a feeling rather like a spring day. A cool breeze blew on him as he walked across the ground. He did not know where he was headed, but he knew it was the right way. He knew that he had to march onwards, whether or not he knew where he was headed. Nobody must know, he thought, but it would have been easier if there were more people there, more people taking the same journey like the sea captain described. More people, Jasper thought, to help guide him in the right direction.

He continued to walk onwards, only thinking and staring at the sky. He had forgotten for a moment that he was shackled, and he went to scratch his face and found that he pulled his other hand up. He noticed, also, that his face now sagged a little more and that he was slightly wrinkled. His bruises were still there, but the bristles of unshaven hair on his face now fell a little lower and, instead of sharp and prickly, they were softer. He felt older as well, mentally and physically, as if he had known more than when he was young. It had not been that long since then, but he had learned so much on his journey.

Jasper stared up into the brilliant sky, the same one that had been looming over him throughout his entire journey. The sun was now higher in the sky, and the stars were no longer visible in the daylight. It must be about lunch time, he thought. His stomach rumbled, which indicated that he was correct. At least, he thought, Bill was kind enough to take him in and feed him. He was a lost man, Jasper thought to himself, but not necessarily a bad one. Perhaps, he said to his mind, that's why he was content to just…sail.

A small, dark figure came into view ahead of him. It was off in the distance, but as Jasper became nearer he noticed that it was a large tree. He had no energy left in him to run, so he walked calmly toward the tree. He had grown tired of running on his journey so he decided to move slower. As he walked, he contemplated everything around him. The sun in the sky, the tree up ahead, even the ground. They were things that he had failed to appreciate throughout his whole journey. Jasper had never really learned to appreciate what he had, but he was learning now. He smiled as he walked slowly onwards towards the tree. *Why should I run*, he thought, *when there is so much to see right here?* The destination became less important as he watched the ground in front of him. The destination, he thought, was not of so much importance. He was here for a reason, and he was sure that it had more to do with his journey than with his final destination.

ANTHONY MURKAR – METAMORPHOSIS

If Jasper was correct, anyway, his destination would be right where he started, and if he were to rush to it, what would he have learned? He continued toward the tree, now noticing that it was atop a round patch of grass. There was more than that, though. There was a wrought-iron fence around it, with gates. The very sight of it reminded him of a park where he used to play as a child, and as he approached it, he realized that it was the very same park. The tree he had noticed from so far off was actually the apple tree he had played in as a child, and the old stone posts that held up the gates were intact. Jasper was unaware of how this could be possible, but he did not fret—he had loved that park as a child and was glad to have the opportunity to return to it. Everyone, he thought to himself quietly, should have the chance to return to places of their childhood. At least, he thought, to revisit them in their minds.

Jasper had actually forgotten the park until he approached it very nearly, recognizing the stone posts and the wrought-iron gate. The lawn was now untrimmed, and the old stone posts were crumbling. The apple tree looked almost dead, and the grass quite dry. The gate was rusted. As he walked up to the place and pushed open the gates, they moved aside with relative ease. The gates were smaller than he remembered them being. He was only eleven the last time he had been in the park, and the gate was as high as his head. Now, he thought, the gates reach only my waist. How I've grown. He pitied the place, though he knew it was partly his fault that the park had become like this. He had lost his past, and without him, the place simply eroded in his mind. It had nearly withered completely, as he had forsaken it, and all that was left of it now was its rusted memory. Even now, at this age, he would have been able to appreciate the park, simply sitting on the bench by the apple tree or watching fish in the creek.

Jasper walked up through the park and across the small wooden bridge. He used to watch the fish there, and he did so now. The fish had not left, and the creek that seemed to appear at the edge of the park and disappear into the ground on the other side was as lively as ever. The water flowed and rushed, and small trout fought against the current. He was hungry, but he could not force himself to catch a fish from this creek. Instead, he wandered over to the apple tree. The dried desert ground disappeared behind him as he walked forward, though he did not look back, as he ventured farther into the park. He picked an apple off the tree and began to chew on it. He knew this place very well, though he had tried to forget it. He had done a fairly good job of forgetting it, as well. It pained him to be here—the memories it brought back brought sharp pain to his chest and his throat. He pushed the feelings down as best he could, but now he was forced to confront this past of his.

Jasper ventured still farther into the park, where he saw another wrought-iron gate. This one was higher, taller than him even, and above it was a black arched sign that read "Saint William Cemetery" in gold lettering. He pushed open the gate here, as well, and wandered in. The cemetery was foggy now, like the other side of the lake, though the fog was lifting due to the sun overhead. He continued to walk through the graveyard, picking up the pace as he ventured farther in. He saw the gravestones passing by him in rows as he ran through. His throat became sore and tight, and his eyes became red as they started to well with tears. He picked up speed still, as he knew his destination. Continuing to run farther and farther, he slowed as he reached his destination.

Jasper wiped the tears from his eyes with his chained hands as he walked onward, approaching a gravestone at the end of the pathway he had been following between the rows of other various stones. He walked up to it and fell to his knees. He screamed in terrible emotional agony as he hugged the gravestone. Several seconds passed, and then several seconds more, as he cried and cried, hugging tightly now the gravestone in his arms. He felt alone and lost in this place, the place that he had confined himself to, and though these feelings barraged him, he knew it was time. He had recognized the park because he had ventured there before, and though he had always backed away from the graveyard where he now stood, he knew he had to confront his fears. It was, as he thought, like an apology that was difficult to give. It hurt him deeply, and though he knew this, he knew he would be forgiven. He knew he had always been forgiven—he had never even been forsaken. Jasper had only forsaken himself.

Jasper cried still, holding the gravestone in his arms. "Mother!" he cried. The name on the gravestone read only "Sarah," though he knew whose stone it was. The stone had belonged to his mother, for which he had never fully mourned. Instead, Jasper had withdrawn from society. He had begun doing drugs, many of them, and in the end, his mother found out only days before her death. Jasper had always believed that it was this that killed her; though she had been sick for a long time, she died only when she found this out, though the doctors had told the family that she had been on the mend.

Jasper could remember plainly the day it happened. He had come into he hospital room one day. He had actually been quite disoriented because of the pills he had swallowed shortly before going in; he couldn't bear to see his mother in such a condition any longer. The doctor came in and let her know that she was doing better, and then came out and told him the same thing he had told the family earlier. He had said that she was improving, against all odds.

Jasper could barely remember the doctor's words. His eyes were red and pained, and he could barely stand. He wandered dizzily into his mother's room, where he promptly fell on on the floor. The doctors rushed in and established what was wrong with him right there, in front of his mother. It was as if he knew what was going on, though he was unconscious.

ANTHONY MURKAR – METAMORPHOSIS

His eyes rolled back into his head as the doctors rushed in and put him on a stretcher in front of his now screaming mother. They took him away, and later explained to her that he had suffered a drug overdose and that, if he had not been in the hospital, he would have died.

Jasper never returned to his mother's room, and only days later, she died, despite her improvements. The thing that made him feel the most guilt was what occurred after his mother's death. He had always, since then, felt as if his mother's death was his fault. He did not attend her funeral afterwards. His family shunned him, though they would have welcomed him if they had known his circumstances. The only two who knew of his problems were he and his mother, and of course the doctors who saved him in the hospital. When he didn't show up at the funeral, he felt as if he could never go back to his family. He had avoided all family functions from that day on, spending a little extra on pills, especially on those days, to numb the pain. It was as if he had simply disappeared from the face of the earth, and over time, he had simply faded away.

Jasper became more obsessed with drugs from then on, and he had nearly died four times since. He felt as if he was cursed, cursed to live on and suffer with his wrongs. It was as if he were being punished for it, though he knew any punishment he suffered was his own doing. His life spiraled down from there, and he never made amends with his deceased mother. He knew, though, that now was the time. It was time for him to finally make amends, time for him to come back to the life he had, like a browned leaf in the fall, simply fallen. It was time for him to come back to reality, and time for him to learn what he needed to learn from this expedition.

Jasper cried more yet, eyes in his hands, until he felt like a sponge that had been squeezed dry of water. He pushed himself up to his knees and rolled over before he promised himself that he would make amends when he returned. He stood up to his feet before he continued onto the gate at the other end of the graveyard. He wandered onward, simply moving forward. He had learned that, in this journey, as long as he continued to move forward, he would end up where he needed to be.

By the time he had reached the gate, Jasper became aware of the fact that the fog was nearly completely gone. The sun had cut through it. It was like an axe to a log, and all that was left were the two sides—one with and one without fog. He continued to the gate opposite where he had come in. He walked through the gate, staring at the ground. He stared at the ground for the simple reason that it was what caught his attention most. It was not grass, it was mud. His spine iced like a puddle of water in January when he thought of more fighting. There was more fighting for him, though, and he knew it. He would be getting more dirty, he was sure of it, though he did not know why.

Jasper took his first step out into the mud, and nearly lost his boot into it. The mud was not like the other mud, which was often only a thin blanket on top of a hard surface. This mud, instead, made him sink. On his second step, he did lose a boot. He was left walking through the mud in his bare feet within minutes. He continued on, though, marching through the mud confidently. He was no longer hungry, having had an apple to eat from the tree in the park, and he was in no pain, emotional or physical, since his exit from the graveyard.

Jasper, still wearing his striped outfit from prison, walked on for more time yet. His heart was beating and his lungs felt as if they were on fire. Jasper never slowed down, though. In fact, he moved only faster. He wandered through the foggy, muddy atmosphere for an hour, at least. He could feel the mud squishing underneath his bare feet and between his toes. Finally, sitting down in the mud to catch his breath, he looked around. It looked like the battlefield, but there were no bunkers or blast craters. It smelled like old potatoes or rotting food. He felt sick just breathing it in. The worst part of it, he thought, was that breathing it in couldn't be avoided. It became more unpleasant as he moved onwards, and before long he was lost in the fog. He began to feel as though he had lost himself yet again, sitting in a pile of mud in the fog, and he was so tired. Jasper laid down, feeling the mud underneath his head, and closed his eyes. Jasper thought to himself, *this will all go away if I close my eyes.* He opened his eyes again only to find himself lying there in the mud in his prison robes.

Sitting up now, Jasper screamed. He could hear his voice echoing in the night; there was nobody there. The frustration welled up inside of him. He yelled once more, but there was no reply. He tripped through the thick mud, landing face first in it. Lying down on the ground, pulling himself out of the mud, Jasper rolled over onto his back and stared up at the sky. *What a shithole*, he thought, *why am I here? What purpose has this served?* For a brief moment, staring at the sky, Jasper thought he saw the faces of those in the audience, including the old woman who had brought him in. "How could this be?" he asked out loud, almost expecting somebody to answer. "How can this place be?"

Who took care of him now, but himself? Jasper had nobody; he had driven them all away. One by one, his addictions grew, and with each new addiction he lost somebody else. He spoke out loud to himself. "If I get out of here, I'll make things right." A sudden burst of confidence grew inside of him, and he decided that he had to move onward. He saw the most brilliant arrangement of stars in the sky. The brilliant stars he remembered seeing as a child were there once more. He saw magnificent reds and greens in the sky, and more stars than he could count. Stars, planets, nebulas. How I wish, he thought, that I could watch the stars with my mother once more.

The sight of the stars made him relax. *I've been feeling sorry for myself,* Jasper thought. *What am I doing? I need to just pull myself up and march out of here. I'll make it back. I know I will. I have to.* Jasper rolled over to his side, then lifted himself up onto his shins and then, finally, he stood up. He was tipsy and dizzy, tired, and now becoming hungry again. *Come on*, he said to himself, *no more of this. No self pity.* He dragged himself onward, one bootless, muddy step at a time.

Marching through the fog, with the brilliant night sky above, Jasper noticed a lump on the ground. Desperately he ran toward it, as fast as humanly possible, under such circumstances. The lump is a person on the ground, a man. "Hey!" Jasper yelled as he approached. "Hey! You!" His heart was beating with excitement as he approached the man. *Perhaps this man will know a way out of here*, Jasper thought to himself.

Running towards the man, Jasper saw the thing's face and gasped. The flesh had all rotted off one side of the man's face, pieces of bone could be seen. The man looked up at Jasper from his position, and Jasper looked down at him, dumbfounded. The man held out a cup toward Jasper. "Can you spare any change?" Jasper felt around in his pockets for some change, but he was no longer in his regular clothes and he had nothing. "Sorry, I don't have anything." Jasper said disgustedly.

The beggar also looked disgusted, as if he thought Jasper was lying to him. "Come on, please. I have no family, I have nothing. I can't get a job, I'm disabled. Please, I need help."

75

Jasper felt around, and finally found a five-cent piece in the pocket of his white and black striped robe, which was now caked with dried mud. He threw the coin down into the man's cup, his chains clinking as he did so. "Thanks, mate." The beggar gave Jasper a smile, and Jasper smiled back.

Feeling a tap on his shoulder, Jasper turned around to find another beggar behind him. "Can you spare a quarter?"

"I'm sorry," Jasper replied, "I have no money."

He heard a voice from behind, and he turns back to the beggar sitting on the ground. "What do you mean? You just gave me a nickel!" Jasper was shocked at the abruptness of the beggar, given his generosity, and the other beggar was now grabbing his arm.

He looked down to see a bony hand clutching onto his arm. "Come on, friend!" the beggar said. Jasper grabbed the hand, which came apart in his grip.

Jasper yelled and ran, tripping again in the mud as he moved away from the beggars. He could see them disappearing in the fog behind him. The fog, he knew, was not his fog; it was theirs. They were lost there, though their fog was obscuring his vision as well. Looking up from the mud, he saw a crutch sticking out of the mud and a bony leg, covered in rotten skin. The smell of the beggar nearly made him spill the contents of his stomach, and he realized that this was the smell he had noticed earlier. He pulled himself up briskly and continued to run, distancing himself from the beggars as much as possible.

As Jasper ran from the beggars, he passed more and more. The farther he ran, the more of them appeared, and soon enough, they outnumbered him so greatly that he could no longer avoid them. They closed in the sides first and, soon, he was running between two rows of beggars. They sprouted up from the ground. Some of them were missing legs, some had no arms, and all smelled of rotting flesh. One with no legs at all sprouted from the ground directly in front of him standing on two crutches, an old paper cup taped to one of the crutches. Jasper's heart pounded harder and harder, his breath becoming more shallow, and his vision clouding. He became hot and anxious as he was slowly closed in by the rotting beggars who now surrounded him completely. They closed in on him quickly now, making him scream louder and louder as they begged for money. As he looked up, now, he saw that none of them bore faces, though they had just moments before. He screamed and yelled with great fright as they closed in on him.

Jasper was now completely closed in, being pushed and shoved by the beggars, as he yelled agonizingly. A head with no face came level with his, and he heard the words "Change! Change! Give us money!" screamed viciously in his ears, coming from every direction.

"I have none!" he yelled. "I've given all I have to give! No more!" The ground beneath him began to soften, and Jasper slid down into the mud, knee deep, unable to move as the beggars grabbed at his clothes.

He slid even deeper, and the ground beneath him seemed to harden. The mud thickened and began to turn solid before drying out instantaneously and hardening him completely in place. He was stuck there briefly, only his head and chained hands sticking out above the ground, but soon the hardened mud started to crack as the ground shook. The mud which now held him captive then seemed to loosen beneath him as it crumbled. He fell through, letting out one final yelp as he plummeted downwards. Looking above him, he could see a group of faceless heads peering at him as the roof above him sealed itself. The last thing he heard was the sound of his own body hitting the ground, and the last thing he saw was a normal human face looking at him, eyes shining in the dark, illuminated by the light of a candle.

CHAPTER EIGHT

YHWH

Jasper awoke to the sound of praying. It was an odd sound—prayer was something he usually associated with silence—and it was suspiciously ominous. At first, he stared only up at the ceiling. Then, as his eyes became accustomed to the light, he sat upright. His head was more painful than it had been before—he thought he might have landed on it—and he raised his hands to his head. He could hear chanting and prayers. There were many people on carpets worshipping, and there were others huddled in circles holding rosaries. Some of them held the Japa Mala, or prayer beads, something that Jasper remembered the name of only by chance. There were men in Turbans, and Catholic priests, or men of the cloth, along with several nuns scattered among the crowd. He suddenly realized that he was in a cave.

The cave was made of a brown stone, a kind of sandy color actually, and was lit by several fires. There were people gathered around the fires, praying, and there were also several torches stuck into the ground. There was a small pond of water, which shimmered in the sunlight that could be seen through a crack in the cave's roof. It was an odd place, and there were several things in the cave that made no sense at all to Jasper.

The first of these things, and the one that seemed most important to Jasper, was a door. There was even a wooden doorframe there, curiously placed within the stone. The door itself was also wooden, which had a brass handle and a glass window, which one could not see through because it was obstructed by newspaper. On the door, in old scratched-up black letters, were the letters YHWH. Jasper recognized it as the name used to refer to God in the Bible. Jasper didn't believe that a cave such as this could house someone as prestigious as his holiness.

He stood up and walked over to a group of people sitting around a fire. There was a person doing a rosary quite quickly and quietly, and several others around a fire. Many of them were just talking in low voices amongst themselves. The people all looked quite old, though Jasper guessed that he probably looked fairly old now, himself. He approached the group and sat down by the fire, and their eyes all followed him. "Excuse me," he started, "but would it be too optimistic to ask if any of you knew where we are?" They continued to stare for a moment before an elderly priest in a traditional black priest's outfit spoke up. "You're in the waiting room, my son. God's waiting room." Jasper looked quizzically at the priest, who offered further explanation. "You see that door over there?" the priest said, indicating the door in the stone marked 'YHWH.'

"Yes," replied Jasper, "I was wondering about that." He smiled at the priest, though the smile he expected back from the priest never came.

"God is through there."

Jasper's smile faded. He wondered if he had he made it to the end of his journey. *Is this my final destination?* he pondered. He looked at the priest with a look of disbelief. "So, why are we out here, then?" Jasper asked, expecting to corner the man.

"You may enter whenever you're ready. We, out here, have decided not to enter as of yet. I, myself, believe that I will enter either heaven or hell upon opening the door, but none of us really knows for sure. We can't know until we open the door, so I'm preparing myself, like everybody else out here. I want to have the best chances possible."

Jasper stared into the priests eyes. "How long have you been out here?"

The priest looked back into Jasper's eyes solemnly, staring for a moment before giving his answer flatly. "Seven years. I have been here praying for forgiveness for seven years." The man seemed almost proud of the time he had spent asking for forgiveness.

"What do you need to be forgiven for?" Jasper asked curiously.

"I don't know, really, but I know I need to be forgiven. I don't want to be punished when I go through."

"Well are you ever going to go through?" Jasper questioned provokingly.

"I would prefer it if you left, please." The priest said harshly. Jasper felt that he was not wanted, so he stood up and walked several steps away. He walked in a circle for several minutes, thinking. "Will I go to hell if I go through that door?" He asked himself repeatedly. He felt afraid of going to hell, but it was not enough to provoke him into staying for seven years praying for forgiveness. "I know what I've done wrong, I know my mistakes," he told himself. "And it's time to find out. I need to know why I'm here." Jasper walked in the direction of the door sternly and unwaveringly, determined to find out what was on the other side.

Several eyes followed Jasper, and the people began to stand as he marched onwards. The crowd followed closely behind him as he neared the door, the entire hoard of them staring greedily and enviously at him and following, in order to try to get a glimpse of what was through the door. He ignored them and, when he reached the door, he turned the handle. He could hear the violins from the orchestra playing a fast song, though they were still out of sight, plucking and strumming viciously, as he approached the door. The song sped up as he neared the door and, when he turned the handle, the song reached a terrific climax. The faces peering over him for a view through the door watched as he slipped inside, and the music stopped.

There was an immense silence, and Jasper could see faces staring at him as he stepped out onto the stage. There was a large black desk in the spotlight at center stage, and the crowd was quite dark and silent. Only their were eyes illuminated by an eerie light. There was a man of small stature sitting at the desk. He looked to be a homeless man, dressed in tattered clothes and with a dirty looking beard. His eyes were deep and knowledgeable, Jasper could see, and his face looked as if it had been worn by the hardships of many lives. Jasper recognized him as the Tenor from the beginning of the show. The stage was still silent, and all that could be heard was the sound of Jasper's bare feet on the wooden stage and the sound of his shackles clinking as he moved. There was an empty chair in front of the desk, and Jasper approached it. The man's eyes followed him the whole way.

As Jasper reached the desk, the man spoke. "It's a shame, isn't it? So many people used to make the journey here. Even of the hundreds who reach my waiting room, very few ever venture into my office." Jasper looked at him confusedly, and then at the crowd whose eyes now focused on him. "Don't worry," the man said, "they can't hear you. Everybody watches the show, but few really get right into it."

"Where am I?" Jasper asked. "Have a seat," the man said, "I'll explain what I can." Jasper did as he was asked and sat in the chair.

"Where am I?" Jasper repeated.

The man smiled. "You're in hell, Jasper." Jasper's face remained stern as he stared at the man. "You're also in heaven, though, so no need to worry." Jasper still stared, as if he were in shock. He was unable to move after hearing those words, almost as if he was stunned by his own confusion.

After a few seconds, though, he gathered himself and spoke. "I don't understand," he said quietly, almost inaudibly, in the low, tired, and beaten-sounding voice of someone in his position.

"Well, Jasper, think of it this way. I'm everything. I'm God, but I am also Satan. When you steal, you feel it inside. That's hell. When you give somebody a present, you feel it too. I feel it. That's heaven."

Jasper loosened up slightly, breaking contact with the man's eyes for a moment to look at the crowd who stared awkwardly into space. He felt odd sitting on the stage beneath their gaze, still bewildered by the sudden change in atmosphere. He felt like a soldier who had woken to find himself at home, lying in bed.

"You want to know why you're here," the man asked, "and I can tell you."

Jasper looked at him again. "I want to know why I'm here," Jasper stuttered tiredly, "and I want to know how I can get back." The man laughed. "I like you, Jasper. Call me God." The man stood up and gestured for Jasper to come. "I want to show you something" he said. God motioned again for Jasper to come, and he stood up from his chair. Jasper followed God down a set of steps to the front of the stage and walked down. They went out through the front and into the crowd, who were still rigidly focused on the now empty stage. "Look at them," God said, "they're so immersed in what's in front of them that they forget to look at what's around them." He waved his hand in front of a person's eyes, but their rigid glare refused to move from the stage. "And, in the end, they can't even see what is right here." He motioned up at the ceiling. "Look at the stars up there, Jasper. They're so beautiful."

Jasper looked up. "What does this have to do with anything?" Jasper questioned.

"I'm glad you asked, Jasper. I don't want you to be like them. I don't want you to miss the things that are really right in front of you. I want you to be free."

Jasper stared at him bluntly. "I was free," Jasper replied sorely, "before you brought me here."

God laughed. "Jasper," he said, "you weren't free. You were shackled, like you are now." Jasper looked down at his hands. "I'm sorry," God started again, "but you'll have to undo your own chains. All I can do is give you a nudge in the right direction, like I did by bringing you here." Jasper knew what the man meant.

"So is that it? I get out of my chains?" Jasper asked.

God smiled. "No, unfortunately not. You have to free yourself entirely." Jasper didn't understand. "Free myself?" he asked.

"Yes," God replied, "free yourself. Come, we've got so much to talk about, this can wait."

They walked back up to the front of the stage, where God sat on the steps. He patted the step beside him and indicated that Jasper should sit beside him. "Come now," he said, "I don't bite." Jasper reluctantly sat beside him on the step. "Jasper," God said, "I'm not going to lie to you. I don't do that. I'm actually very blunt and frank. You make your own existence, Jasper, and what you've made for yourself is hell. That's what it is, Jasper. I know you feel guilty about so many things, but you don't need to."

"But—" Jasper started, but he was cut off by God, who waved his finger in the air for a moment to silence Jasper.

"I know what you're going to say, Jasper. And, as I said, I won't lie; it was wrong. It wasn't your fault, though, Jasper."

Jasper felt sad and apologetic. He fought to keep himself from tearing up.

"Let it go, Jasper. It was her time—you had nothing to do with it." Jasper couldn't hold it in any longer. His eyes welled up immediately, and God held him as they sat on the steps. God comforted him as he cried.

"I'm sorry!" Jasper yelled as he wept. After several minutes, he let go of God. He wiped his red eyes on his dirty robes. He gathered himself before starting again.

"I need to know. How can I get home?"

God smiled. "You'll be glad to know you aren't dead." Jasper had not considered before that he may have already died. *Is it possible?* he asked himself in his mind.

"Yes," God said, "it is possible."

Jasper, surprised that God knew what was going through his mind, replied out loud. "So how do I get out?"

ANTHONY MURKAR – METAMORPHOSIS

God smiled once more. "It's easy, free yourself from your prison."

Jasper didn't understand. "I'm not in a prison, though. I'm no prisoner." Jasper tried to explain this to God.

"If you weren't a prisoner," God said, "you wouldn't be wearing those chains or those robes. If you can just free yourself, Jasper, then you've won your war."

Suddenly, God was gone, and Jasper was no longer on stage. The faces of the audience had vanished, replaced by heavy steel bars that sprouted before Jasper's eyes. The wooden floor beneath his feet changed to concrete, and the desk that lay behind him on the stage lowered and turned into a bed. The lights above dimmed, and Jasper found that he was in a prison cell. It was pitch black outside, and Jasper was standing at the front. The small bunk bed in the corner housed a second person who slept on the bottom. He felt tired and hopeless, as if he had been drawn suddenly from a safe place and thrown into a pool of shallow water among hungry alligators. He wrapped both of his hands around the cold steel bars in front of him and stared out into the enormous prison, spanning as far as he could see in either direction and with floors reaching high up into the sky and down many flights to the ground.

CHAPTER NINE

Breaking Free

Jasper had no idea how to free himself. He couldn't do anything, he thought, locked in that cell. He sat down in the corner on the concrete floor. He rubbed his eyes while he thought to himself quietly about his escape. He could see a few rays of light, now, through a small barred window to the back of his cell. The sun was coming over the hills off in the distance. He could still see the faces of the audience watching him. Watching, but doing nothing.

It was only a minute or so before the sun rose completely over the hills. It must have been early morning, he thought. The lights in the dark prison came on shortly after, and a buzzer sounded. He sat down on the floor and watched out of his cell as several faceless guards walked up the stairs to his level of cells. The prison was expansive, but the guards appeared only seconds after the bell sounded, all marching in tune up the stairs. He was almost expecting them to open his cell when they passed, pausing for a moment to observe him, but they continued. The guards seemed to be just walking up and down the rows of cells, taking no particular notice of the prisoners who now rose from their beds. From the bed across from his own cell, Jasper could see a faceless being in a suit rise from his bed. The man held a briefcase, and he sat down on an invisible chair. The main removed, from his suitcase, several papers and a pen.

Looking at the other cells, Jasper saw similar occurrences. In one cell a man dressed like a judge sat atop in an invisible court waving his gavel at people who weren't there. He then proceeded to pound the gavel on a surface, which was also not visible, though Jasper could hear the sound it was making. A cell off to the right of the judge suddenly grabbed his attention. A man, dressed also in a suit, yelled uncontrollably at the wall only inches from his face. To the right of that, Jasper saw a man dressed almost like he had been only a day or two previously, looking quite homeless. He held a cup out and thanked the air in front of him every so often.

From behind him, Jasper heard the ruffling of sheets. Another in coveralls, carrying a hammer, rose from the bed. He sipped something from a mug which wasn't there for only a moment before placing it down and picking up his hammer. The man came towards Jasper and swung the hammer toward his head. Jasper ducked out of the way, falling onto his back and pulling himself away from the man using whatever strength was left in his chained hands. The man continued to pound away at the wall with his hammer, before lifting an imaginary nail up to the wall and hammering at it again. He felt as if he suddenly understood, as if he knew what it was about. He couldn't frame his understanding into words—that seemed impossible to him—but he felt as if he just….*knew.*

Jasper stared at the man, who continued this motion over and over. Jasper stood up and walked over to the man. "Hello?" He said. The man did not move. "Hello!" He yelled. The man still stood still, not moving. The guards seemed to not hear him either. He waved his hands in front of the man's eyes, as God had done to those in the audience earlier, and found that the man was completely nonresponsive.

Jasper stared for a minute, almost expecting something different to happen. Nothing different did happen though, and by the time the sun had risen far above the hills, the man was still hammering away at the wall. Jasper frowned angrily as his face contorted in anger, and he ran up to the man and pushed him. He pushed and pushed, but the man didn't budge. Jasper's feet slid as he attempted to move the construction worker, but the man refused to move.

Jasper yelled in frustration, screaming incessantly. The carpenter suddenly stopped, and the faceless beast came walking towards him. Jasper met the man at eye level, and the gruesome beast of a person breathed heavily through his face onto Jasper's. Jasper grew fearful, and he screamed once more. The shrill sound of a man screaming pierced the prison—it was Jasper. The construction worker continued to come at Jasper, who was now against the wall with two hands wrapped around the bars. The man pressed heavily on his back, his face staying near Jasper's face. The beast's hands reached around Jasper, grasping almost randomly at his face with great strength.

90

"I don't want it!" he screamed, "Let me out!"

Jasper pulled as hard as he could, pulling for his life. His heart beat and his palms grew sweaty and red. His head became full of pressure and his vision clouded, and suddenly his chains began to deteriorate. "Let me be free!" He regurgitated loudly, screaming almost agonizingly. The bonds around his wrists fell from his hands, and the bars that Jasper was pulling at began to bend under the force of his strength. At first, they bent only a little bit, but then they began to bend completely and easily around his hands. The strings of the orchestra began strumming almost at random, creating an enormously loud and high-pitched screeching and thrashing sound, which increased in volume and speed as time progressed.

The bars melted down onto his hands as he pulled, falling out of the concrete as it crumbled and melted. The guards vanished and the prisoners vanished. Suddenly, it was dark, and the prison melted around Jasper, coating him in the melted substance. He was screaming viciously, now, the image of the bricks reflecting on the surface of his skin. The prison was visible, and then the horizon. The stage, and then the cave and, back farther past the park. The sea captain was visible, laughing as he puffed a cigar, and then the prison yard from which he had escaped. Jasper fell over, putting his hands to his face. His hands stuck, though, and he couldn't remove them from his face. The old woman could be seen, now, waving her plaid umbrella through the air. Jasper was stuck, almost

91

caving inwards, screaming at the top of his lungs as loud and hard as he could.

Suddenly, Jasper awoke, screaming. He felt his face, and felt his hands. There were no chains, and he was no longer old—he was his former self. He looked around in fright, quickly. There was nobody around him. He was sitting alone in the theatre, screaming to himself in his seat. The stage was empty, and the curtains were drawn back to reveal the large desk and two empty chairs. The orchestra was now gone, and it was silent in the theatre. The stars that had once coated the top of the stage were gone, and the roof appeared to be only comprised of what a normal roof would be comprised of.

Jasper felt himself to make sure he was real, before standing up and running out of the theatre. He pushed his way past the familiar doorman who held a stack of ticket stubs, and found that the street was busy with people and cars. There were people lined up for the next show around the sides of the buildings, but he noticed that the door between the two lines still remained quite empty. At each door a busy man stood arguing loudly with another person. He stepped towards the edge of the sidewalk and looked around frantically, seeing nothing familiar. He walked down to a corner of the building.

Feeling around in his pocket, Jasper found his ticket. It was labeled 9:30 PM. He tapped a man on the shoulder, and he immediately turned around. "Excuse me," Jasper asked, "but would you mind telling me what time it is?"

"It's…9:20," was the reply. The show hadn't started yet? Jasper was unsure what was going on, but he was beginning to feel calm. He gathered himself and stood at the door. To his left, Jasper saw a rather poor looking young man smoking a cigarette at the other end of the building. "Doesn't he know better?" Jasper asked himself.

He looked down at the ticket in his hand, which still had its stub. "Hey you!" Jasper called to the man. "Yeah, you. Come here!"

The man looked over at him, and then walked past the line of people towards Jasper repeating, "Excuse me, pardon me," as he walked.

As the young man approached, Jasper began, "Hey, I've got one ticket, and I need to sell it. You willing?"

The young man looked at the ticket. "How much?" he asked.

"The show's starting in ten minutes, people are lined up, and I probably won't sell this ticket if you don't buy it. Make an offer."

The young man pulled a crumpled ten-dollar bill from his pocket and said, "This is all I have."

"Alright," Jasper replied, "Enjoy the show." He handed the ticket over to the young man and walked away with his refund. As he walked, the old woman with the plaid umbrella passed him on the sidewalk and smiled. Jasper smiled back contentedly.